A
MAYBELLINE ROMANCE
FICTION

My First Crush

By
BORA' NYREE

ISBN979-8-88955-874-3

You brought my story to life.

Thank you, Aunty Shaun…

CONTENTS

CHAPTER ONE

Amanda

The only truth about LOVE is when anger masquerades as PASSION.

The streets were barren as I drove to the airport. A lonely tint of red-yellow crossed the skies. The only sign of life was an occasional pair of headlights passing by. It was 5 a.m., but my girlfriend had me stretch my neck out for her. Amanda's constant buzzing of my phone had woken me up. She called and texted every 5 minutes. I had no choice but to get up. Her text messages only read, "Chris, meet me at the airport···ASAP." I had no clue she was at the airport and why she wanted me there and that early. I returned her calls, but they went unanswered. Fearing the worst, I decided to drive there in a panic, suspecting something must have been awfully wrong. To my knowledge, we were not expecting any friends or family members on a flight to town. And even if that was the case, it would've been logical for them to catch a taxi—Uber. I reasoned.

Glass doors swung open as I walked in on a crowd of passengers. Adults pulled and rolled their stuffed bags while kids trailing them screamed for attention. Others were hunched over with backpacks, pushing their way to check-ins and boarding gates. Floors were chaotically organized, escalators jammed to max capacities with hardly any room to stand. The logic behind the invention of escalators was that you stand on them, and it does the walking for you. But that original design hardly worked at this airport. People walked on them, not to mention the countless stumbles I saw in that short period. It was rather amusing. I could not make any sense out of that sensibility. Their patience ran thin.

Lines at the check-ins were worse than at grocery stores the day before Thanksgiving. It felt like a city in a house.

Ringtones—texts, screams of "Mom! Mom," loud intercoms departure—arrival, flight numbers, "Now Boarding," highly mounted monitors flashed images and letters too small to read. In a word, overwhelming. But that was none of my concerns; Amanda was. In my opinion, it was way too early for this kind of commotion. Noise interminable. To be fair, the noise decibels were at par compared to the rubber and tarmac on my way there. I felt sorry for the workers too. They were busy moving trash, giving directions, and constantly changing their plastic gloves to avoid germs. What a life!

My hair had not seen a comb, and my teeth got a quick swoosh of the minted mouthwash about three times to be exact. I wore canvas shorts and Lacoste tennis shoes. Talk about a total mismatch. One could easily tell that I had no plans of going to the public that morning. I thought about my dad, a man given to fashion and trends. He would've hated seeing me in mismatched outfits and not well-kept. A very bad representation of his family, as he would say on many occasions.

Behold! I was met by a familiar pair of blood-shot eyes. Amanda leaned on a pillar, her face flushed red like a piece of scarlet-clothing. I jogged in her direction, dodging perfect strangers and random-things to get to her. I could tell she had been crying by the swelling around her eyes. I hastily braced for whatever she was going to spring up on me. It had been her custom to pull the plug whenever things went down. Not knowing what her issues were that morning, I thought she had gone too far. I had been groomed to rescue a damsel in distress. And if you were to guess it, Amanda was that damsel. She wore the title to the very-tee. And for as long as I had known Amanda, her feelings moved like trade-winds from one extreme to the other. And there was no telling how strong and or in what direction they would swing. I could easily say that she was a spoiled brat, but I hesitated because she was far too calculating for an easy—read like that.

"You—alright?" I gasped for air, looking into her eyes…

"I'm sorry, Chris, I don't want to hurt you," she replied.

She was extremely calm in contrast to the frequency of her earlier missed calls and string—texts. Her sudden composed demeanor made me regret why I had driven there and that fast. Was this a prank? Did she just freak me out for attention? Had I driven like a rickety cannon, risked my life and others for this? But her calmness confirmed my suspicion. Amanda must have rehearsed every—thought and move before I got there. Her mind games never stopped; if she was thinking or talking about anything, it was likely a plot to get something. Attention, money, fun, you name it, she was game. But this time around, I wasn't flabbergasted. Just flat—out upset. I watched Amanda steer her hair behind her ears, concocting how to spill the beans. My intuition had warned me in advance, and I anticipated something like this happening. Over the years, our relationship has been defined by the addiction to chaos. There was no other way to put it. The drama was the glue that kept our relationship going. Every breakup we had was nothing more than a setup for makeup. Strange as it was, something was awfully wrong that morning. She appeared determined to make a drastic change. Her mind was made up. Amanda wasn't as feisty as she usually was whenever we had problems. Not knowing how her new vibe would impact me, I braced myself for the worst and hoped for the best. It felt like separation anxiety. But what choice did I have?

"Okay, so... I'm catching a plane and leaving for a while. I don't know when I'll be back, but don't worry about me or tell anyone. Okay?" She looked at me tensely, needing my affirmation.

"Okay···but why and where are you going?" I asked, watching her face suddenly flash with exasperation at my line of questioning.

"I've been trying to get along with my parents, but···." Her voice trailed off as she ran her hands through her hair again. It was a sure sign of troubled waters when Amanda brushed her hands through her hair. And my cue was on point.

"I don't want to deal with them right now. So··· I'm just leaving." She settled uneasily at the realization that I wasn't buying her sack of lies.

Her emotions swelled out whenever she disagreed with her parents, and I was the dump site. However, that morning, I didn't get that from her. Unlike in the past, she didn't give a detailed line-by-line encounter. There were no elaborations except she was leaving town. Her usual anger had evaporated. Her familiar emotional expressions of angst and disappointment appeared forced.

"Stay with me for a few days; cool down." I was troubled for her safety and wearisome to save the situation.

Rolling her eyes, she said, "That's not gonna solve anything." She was firm.

"And running away is?" I snickered sardonically while guardedly avoiding crossing that magical line.

"I'm sick of going back and forth with them! They don't care about me. I cannot live up to their expectations, and I'm done doing that." She said.

I gave her a hug before she had the fortuitous to let us go. I felt like she was trying to leave more than just her parents behind. I was included in that count too. It was strangely terrifying knowing that Amanda didn't need me anymore.

"But why leave? What am I supposed to do 'til you come back?"' I placed my forehead on hers for assurance.

"If I come back." she muttered.

"Wait, What?" I stepped back, gazed into her eyes, and searched for meaning. My heart stopped, and I tuned—out noises in the background. Things froze in time. She had my full attention. I read both her lips and words in slow motion.

“What’s that supposed to mean? If I come back.” My mind hunted for words. It was ridiculous at best. Her art of creating grand—gestures and dramatic scenes was simply perfect. It was not what she said but how she said it. There was an awkward silence between us. She hankered for attention and waited for my truest reaction. But this move dragged my last nerves. She was literally running away from home! And she hadn’t told me a thing about it until now. I had no idea where she was headed or who she would stay with. For all I knew, Amanda could’ve been leaving the country.

The situation could've been fixed if I had gotten to her on time and calmed her down like I always did. Or so I thought. However, my usual magical wand did not work. She had planned to stir up the pot beyond her normal attention—seeking binge. Expectedly I found myself wedged in her drama again.

A few days earlier, I had contemplated ending this behavior but had hesitated to make that passage. In a way, she beat me to it. I had willingly bailed her out for so long and on numerous occasions. My tolerance had worn out. Had nothing left to feed her crazy—making.

Drama—queen or not, Amanda was my first love. Our vicious cycle of on—off had worn itself out, and the little good we had left slowly vanished to the horizon. This time around, though, things were different and somber for me. She had drawn the *getting out of town card.* As I sorted out our lost-in-translation moment, the intercom—departure announcements emanated. Her flight was ready to board gate 3. She hurriedly congregated her bags for the trip. My mind contested for anything I could say to keep her from parting ways with me to no avail.

"Amanda, wait···" I gripped her arm but couldn't think of anything to say. And in that instant, I realized my words were not enough to persuade her to stay. She was unbendable. Panic engrossed me at the gullet, and a lump of rage almost choked me. I was troubled but could not express it in civic.

"Chris, you need to forget about me." she said with remorse and a smirk. I hated her countenance, with the whole—lot in me. When people sneer while making irrational choices···it's very impolite. Was this one of those speeches, "*It's not you, it's me?*" I wondered. Truth is, I was being dumped, and helplessly at that.

She vehemently snatched her arm from me and walked away, scrabbling with her bags. I screeched her name! I couldn't hold it in any longer. I blasted from my diaphragm like a siren, but she kept walking to board. She didn't turn around. Not even once. I just stood there, perplexed—sorrowful and awkwardly staring as people turned in my direction. It was obvious things were not well with us.

But since security at the airport is always tight. On high alert, I didn't want any attention, let alone getting TSA agents looking my way. Amanda had taken everything I had. Her. She was my love. All I ever wanted.

***

I plunged into nothingness days that followed. Twenty-four hours was too much to take in all at once. I chunked them down to minutes. One after another. I did everything possible to distract my mind from thinking about her. Played video games, watched movies, exercised, and took long walks. But the real test of my tenacity to move on would come in the middle of the night. Sleepless in Seattle, I had nothing on this…

Everything around me seemed to scream her presence. It was a constant longing for her usual text messages and phone calls. I missed her impromptu show-ups at my place and hearing her say, "Chris! What u—doing?

Open the door." I battled my mind, especially in the evening hours, the usual times she showed up. I missed listening to her day's drama without interruption. Amanda left me with memories, thoughts—more thoughts. I consoled myself that she would knock on the door or send a text. I kept my phone fully charged and on me always. I don't know what was worse for me, the anticipation of hearing from her or the hope that this was a bad dream. My life had submerged into deeper waters of depression; I was drowning bit by bit. On the outside, nothing about my life had changed, but on the inside, the whole thing felt unversed. My phone had scrolls of missed calls and text messages. But none was from her. I had no desire to answer them. Even mom, who hardly called did. Amanda was on my mind. I reminisced about our romance all the way back to high school. Though we had grown up together and from the same neighborhood, my affection for her came gradually over the years. In the beginning, it was the innocence of child's play. I was more of her big brother than a lover. I always took up for her, protecting—providing. Yep providing. I was game if I could steal a few dollars from my mom's purse to buy her chocolate. I must admit, she'd boss me around in the backyard a few times while our mothers laughed at my inability to find perfect hideouts as we played hide and seek.

We enjoyed playing together and going to the malls with our mothers to shop, but it was more like them walking—off their boredom. My fondest memory came when one day while playing our usual hide and seek, I hid under the bed. As expected, Amanda came looking for me. Lighting in the house was deemed. Little did I know that she was afraid of darkness. I stayed under the bed for as long as I could. Frustrated and not wanting to go any further, she called me out. Sensing victory, I hung on just a little longer. But then her voice quickly turned into despair.

"This is not funny!" She was about to walk out when I quickly pulled me by the stomach from under the bed. Horrified at the sudden movement and noises, she screamed at the top of her lungs. I held her tight and reassured her it was me. My girl had fallen apart in fear. She was breathing heavily; her legs went noodles on me. I couldn't let her go for fear she could collapse. I do not know if it was a relief or an instinct, but she kissed my lips, and I kissed her back. We just stood there and held each other. I enjoyed that moment, albeit nervously. I could sense that she was shaken. The kiss felt good and was the first time ever felt a girl's lips on mine. It was a wet kiss and obviously imperfect, but we were young to tell the difference.

I preserved that moisture and did not wipe or touch my lips for long. Nonetheless, we had woken up something in us. It was strangely safe that she needed me. That momentary awkwardness sealed the fate of the tie that would bind us. What adults did in exchange for love and affection, we had just done that—kissed. I never saw Amanda the same way again. I wanted her to be my girl forever. The innocence we once shared was broken. We could no longer play hide and seek like that again. We avoided eye contact whenever our families got together. It was that feeling you get, suspecting someone knows your secret, and you try to avoid them, fearing they might leak it to the public.

From that moment onwards, there was a thickness of tension between us. I didn't know how to break that ice and talk about the kiss or how it felt. I could only master the courage to say, "Hi, Amanda," she seemed to follow my lead, "Hi, Chris." ···and "How are you doing?" She would casually respond with, "Good."

I was certain our parents thought we were growing up and boys wanted to play with boys and vice versa, but the truth was, I had developed feelings for Amanda. A line of innocence had been crossed.

Amanda and I didn't talk freely until later in high school. Our notarized silence was broken by the homework, of all things. She needed help with her math assignment from me. And that's how we broke our self—exiled relationship, albeit in minimal dosages. I never brought up the subject, and she stayed clear. Deep inside, I wanted to tell her how I truly felt. By then, it was too late. Her popularity had soared. She had joined the up en—up crowds at school. Other guys discovered the beauty that once belonged to me. In disappointment, I backed off and hated myself for not saying anything while I had the chance. I wondered if she ever felt the same feelings, I had for her. Sure, being a geek has its ups and downs. It raised my value. Beautiful girls in my grade wanted my help with homework too. Some even sat by my side in class just in case they ran into trouble with school work. Chances were good that I could practically date any girl of my choice. But I held back from connecting with any of them for fear that Amanda would surely be gone forever this time. Was I wrong, stupid, or both? Kids who played sports in school wanted Amanda, and I was left out. My luck came when she got dumped. Yep, I was there to pick up the pieces. That's how our romance blossomed. At the back of my mind, I knew I was that innocuous kid from her home-turf who needed to get out of her friend-zone. We both knew I was her rebound, but we couldn't admit it.

Amanda's breakup was a public fallout at the cafeteria. She saved face with me. Rumors about her attitude and shallow mind had twirled around like a wild-storm. Kids at school called her loose, while others a witch. My big-brother-self had gotten into a few of those fights to defend her honor. I knew Amanda best from home. It was my duty to secure and protect my own. Well, with ulterior motives, of course, but who wouldn't? She was cute! I had amenably confessed my affection using actions without saying the dreaded words, "I like you, Amanda." But that did little to ease my internal frustrations. So, I decided to confide the secret—crush to one of my buddies. He told me not to tell her verbally but use actions, and I did. All those years, Amanda played possum with me. She did not acknowledge my presence or my acts of kindness. And for some reason, my attraction for her grew stronger, not weaker. At the pick of her fame, she dated Brad, the captain of our high school basketball team. Things, however, didn't work-out as she had planned. Brad was too famous and one of the most sought-after dudes by girls in school. The guy practically lived in the gym and only took breaks in between to party. Things went south when Lori, a new-girl who had transferred to our school in the eleventh grade, tickled his fancy. He quickly grew fond of her. To add insult to injury, Lori was much younger and a beauty queen.

Amanda's fame and popularity immediately came into contestation. She hated Lori's competition with a passion. Lori's smart moves quickly earned her the royalty ticket to the upper echelon while Amanda's public value took a tumble. She laid out drama, a fight ensued, and Brad came to Lori's aid instead of Amanda. At that point, it was obvious Amanda was out, and Lori was in. Oh well, but for me, Amanda was the apple of my eye. In a fate of diversified twists, her demise with Brad was my gain. I seized the moment. In my heart, I wanted the chance to date her. I knew we could love each other. I didn't care what kids in school said. Giving up on the girl of my dreams was not an option. So, I wrote a note and secretly dropped it in her book bag. It read, "Amanda, I like you. Will you be my girl friend?" I waited anxiously for her response. Three days later, while getting on the school bus, she turned around and said, "Yes." I was stunned by how she used only one word, and there it was our first date.

“Can you take me to the movies this weekend?” Stared at me with a puppy—look.

“Sure, why not,” I answered, smiling like I had just seen the heavens open.

And the rest was history···

I would later learn that her decision to date me was purely based on avoiding the shame of being dumped and lonely. Brad’s rejection did a number on her. Sad, I know.

This is how the scoop dropped on my lap. It was a Friday night at the movies, and Amanda and I were entangled in a frenzied argument; she lost her cool in the heat of the moment and blasted out the bitter—truth about us. Low does not describe the deflation my ego went through. I never recovered. She was loud. The whole world gasped in disbelief.

If grounds could open, I would be willing to be buried right then and there.

She regretted telling me the truth, but it needed to be said. Our relationship took a beating by that confession. My ego was crinkled. She was no longer my dream girl but a friend who happened to be a girl. I did not want us to breakup. My feelings for her were deep and strong. There was no denying that reality, and I couldn't move passed it. We were like scrambled eggs without a cook. From there on, I second—guessed her devotion and love throughout our dating. Finding out she was with me because she felt sorry for me did not sit well. Especially when she was the one that had been dumped by Brad. We were never the same. Our relationship's crescendo plateaued and went downhill to the gorge, and without breaks, we plummeted. We broke up and got back together several times over the years. Our excitement needed a breakup to ignite a hook-up. On-and-off cycles turned out to be too familiar territory. So, when she decided to leave Luce, the city we both called home, I knew her decision had a finality to it.

Amanda's way out was to hermit herself from her parents, the city, and me. I felt cheated in this relationship; I had gone too far above and beyond where most guys would've given up. I never got the admiration I merited from her. On many occasions, out of optimism, I held onto hope that she would change her ways, but it never happened. Seceding from me was not my desire. I had underestimated my emotional ability to withstand a breakup. Her ploy of needing space and time was nothing more than a scheme to run away. How could I make any sense of this predicament? Did she suppose I would forget about her just like that? Of course not, but she did it anyway. She only thought about herself. I wasn't staggered, just stunned at my own realization. She was a big part of my life, and the breakup took a heavy toll on me.

***

The dead of the winter didn't help either; it only added to my misery. Her absence was an endless nerve-wracking reality. While we dated, I always found something to complain about; I thought she was too much and overboard. Now that she had left, I was surprised by how much I needed and loved her. I could not tell if this was a form of addiction or looking at my past in rosy colors, but I needed Amanda back. I kept busy, kept moving, occupied my emptiness with frequent visits to uncle Joe's café. It was my home away from home. I felt better and rejuvenated being there. Even though transitorily as always. But it held a special place in my heart.

Uncle Joe was the closest thing to normal as far as family went. Being my dad's best friend, he played the integral role of a god—father. He took it seriously too. Both men had ventured into business with different aspirations. My dad became a real estate developer, while uncle Joe ran a café shop in our neighborhood. Dad's success in real estate meant that we were financially worry—free. But the trauma that came with it wrecked our family. We hardly functioned as a unit. He was gone for weeks and months at a time. I was accustomed to not seeing him often. I recall one time, he came home very excited with the news that he had acquired a property downtown. It was a 10-story building, and he was to renovate it for occupancy. I was happy for him, but he never understood that all I wanted was to spend some time with him. He could've taken me to some of those ventures but chose not to. He had zoned me in the little boy—club instead. In his eyes, I was that kid that needed to ride a tricycle. I guess that's why he expected me to stay home with mom and hardly knew I was grown, driven and dated. On the other hand, Uncle Joe had been there for me all those years.

Dad missed the chance to help me un-clutter the pile of struggles a young adult was going through. My dating life was in the tank, and I desperately needed him for advice. He was a no—show; our only connection came from watching his archived video tapes. He was a terrific swimmer. I give him that. It ran in our blood. We all loved the waters, period. Sometimes I thought that swimming could've been why we lived in coastal states. I had lost count of the many times we went to the ocean on weekends. The legend himself, grandpa, set precedence. He held a few titles under his belt. Naturally, my dad inherited the sport and did very well too. He was not disappointed. Being the second generation, I was not about to lose our heritage. Obviously, to feel closer and keep the family tradition, I took on the sport for myself. With time, my passion for the sport grew immensely. So, breaking up with

Amanda left a void that only swimming could fill.

I immersed myself in it and was determined to be a champion. Nothing would stop me. I had to shine among the stars. Crowds would scream my name. I aimed far beyond state competitions and tournaments. I wanted to be an Olympian. Winning a gold medal was added to my bucket list. The State's Elite Swimming Program recruited me. In the beginning, ESP proved harder than I had thought. It was intense. Had to wake up every morning at 4, jog a few miles, and then hit the gym for about an hour. If that wasn't hard enough, shortly after breakfast, training sessions started.

We trained for hours at a time. Afterward, we had a group lunch before breaking off for the day. I was too exhausted for anything else other than a nap. My coach did not make excuses kindly. He ensured I worked out and trained hard. The first two months were the hardest for me. Initially, my concentration was distracted by the breakup with Amanda.

Additionally, my body was not ready for rigorous activities. It took a while to adapt to my new routine. So, one afternoon, while drinking a protein shake after training, it just dawned on me that I had not thought about Amanda. Sure, she crossed my mind. But unlike this, I had no feelings of missing her or hurting from the breakup. It felt surprisingly good. My life was taking on a new shape. So, I decided to train even harder. I set new goals. I gained more muscle and looked, well—herculean. The new diet worked out perfectly for my body type. My performance improved. I got stronger. Looking back, I was in the best shape of my life. The geek look that once defined me had disappeared. I got rid of my old wardrobe and hairstyle. Those binocular glasses I had worn for an eternity were out the window. Ladies had taken notice. While guys were hitting on girls, I was getting the exact opposite. They were hitting on me. Brad's well-kept secret was out; to be popular, all it took was sports and looks.

Izzy, Uncle Joe's niece, was the only girl I hung out with and at their home whenever I visited. She was beautiful and lively. Though heavily guarded emotionally, I liked her very much. Don't get me wrong, Izzy was not new to me. We had known one another since middle school. She moved to Luce from

Florida to live with her relatives' uncle Joe and aunty Madelyn. At that time, my eyes were fixated on Amanda. We friend-zoned each other. But in my heart of hearts, I was attracted to her.

Dating or not, Izzy's mind was difficult to read. Her intentions were securely hidden. She didn't have much to say most of the time. It was in the eleventh grade when she had just disappeared from School. The next time I saw her was at Uncle Joe's café and working as a barrister. Izzy lived with Grandma Isabel, aunty Madelyn's mother. She was a great chess player too. Uncle Joe could not beat her. I was the only one who won whenever we played. Yeah, the joke was that she let me win. But Izzy and I knew I was too tough to beat. It was one of those things the inner circle knew and never shared. Treating her like a god—sister was very hard for me. I wanted more between us. Of course, I understood family values. Uncle Joe and aunty Madelyn were my god parents. But we were not related by blood. That should've not been a factor to consider if I had chosen to date Izzy, right? I was determined to close the gap and hopefully ask her out on a date. Of which I did.

One afternoon, I invited Izzy to my practice sessions at the community swimming pool. Training with no end in sight had become my tradition, maybe an obsession. She agreed and joined me at the pool later that day.

"Hey, Izzy!" I waved at her. She sat at the far end of the bench across from where I stood by the diving board. I splashed some water on my chest and face, jumped in the pool, and normalized my body temperature before jumping out. This was my routine before training sessions. In addition, I wanted to flex, and show off my physique to the girls that came to the pool to swim or just to cool off. In my mind, I wanted to see if I could get a reaction from Izzy. Did she like me? She hid her emotional expressions so well.

Besides agreeing to my invitation, I had nothing else to go by. The dude in me wanted a relationship with her so bad, even though I risked ruining our friendship. The reality of getting in trouble with Uncle Joe was in my mind. But that wasn't enough to stop me from pursuing her. What else could go wrong? I had confided in Uncle Joe about my relationship with Amanda over the years. As a man, he was able to understand my plight. I reasoned.

Don't get me wrong now; his family immensely supported me. They kept their commitments from the date they became my god parents, even though my mother did not readily accept their kindness. She took it with a grain of salt. It must have stemmed from the fact that they had no children and poured all their love into me. That must have sparked jealousy or possessiveness in my mother. They didn't have as much money as my dad, but they gave me more. Every child's dream is to spend quality time with his or her parents. My mother was hurt by it. Partly because my dad encouraged them, and they were eager to fulfill that responsibility. I think everybody knew they had a void in their marriage. For starters, dad seemed not to care about Uncle Joe and aunty Madelyn's affinity for me. The emptiness my mom experienced was hard to describe in words. It was something one could easily feel but not explain. It's like she wanted dad to succeed but rescinded him when he did. On many occasions, I heard her tell people that all she had was his money and not him. Earlier in their marriage, she chronically complained about him not making enough money. Confusing, I know, but that was our story.

Whenever aunty Madelyn came over or invited us to an outing, mom came up with every excuse in the world not to go. I guess she avoided feeling like her husband was never there or that she wasn't good enough. I didn't dwell on it that much. Simply because my dad was going to do what he wanted to do anyways. In his mind, he was a provider and an adventurer. If you asked him, mom needed to sort out her life. As for me, I was not about to let the world pass me by. I had resolved to love my dad. I adjusted to accepting him just the way he was. But I must confess that the thought that my dad avoided confrontations with mom's manipulative tendencies closely resembled my battles with Amanda.

Not to be biased, but I had noticed that whenever mom wanted something from dad, she fought him tooth and nail. On several occasions, she told dad that other men treated their wives better than he was. I don't think she understood how upsetting that made him feel. He was my father, and I was proud of him. Even though he continually starved me of quality time. When mom was happy, she preferred to hang out with her friends instead of him. At first, he took in that rejection without retaliation. But I guess he must have had enough overtime. For he rarely came around, and when he did, he did not stay for long. They were separated without separating.

One time I overheard him complain about his mom pushing him away. I was too young to understand it then. But from the little I could gather, they fought over money; since then, my dad has always worked. I could see why dad submerged himself in business from that vintage point. I guess we got money and lost him.

My passionate affinity for swimming may have developed as a coping mechanism to escape the drama at home. Was I duplicating my father with Amanda? Maybe but Amanda was a different case altogether. I reasoned those men needed an external purpose to combat falling in love with any woman. Emotional hurt was no joke. Whatever my dad meant to mom and me was for good. I concluded.

Uncle Joe and his family continued to support me though it all. They were my biggest cheerleaders. Mom hardly attended my swimming events. Aunt Madelyn took more interest in my swimming, though. Never missed a tournament. It was personal for her. I was her informally adopted son. That's why I hesitated to really talk with Izzy. I didn't know how the family would react. Uncle Joe counseled me on many things young adults my age needed. Well, in his mind, I was eighteen even though I had cracked my early twenties. He took time out, listened to my dreams, and helped me see things differently. He became the father I never had in so many ways. I valued his time with me more than anything in the world. Through him, I saw a man's world. He was a good listener, especially when it came to my dreams and ideas. Because of him, I was invigorated never to give up.

A few weeks earlier, while having our usual man—talk, he said, "Chris, I want you to work at the shop with me."

"Uncle, you know I have no experience with this kinda stuff," I replied cautiously, not to disappoint him.

"Think about it this way, son, you've got your life on track now. Things are much better than they once were a few months ago. You've got a passion for swimming. You are gonna be great. But you need discipline and accountability." His tone went low and firm.

"What do you mean by discipline and accountability?" I was confused.

"Remember when you said you waited for Amanda to call for days? That was a lack of accountability. You allowed Amanda to control your life. Even though you hated how things were between the two of you, she became the center of your life⋯." He reeled his fishing rod in and cast it back out to the waters. The pond he fished at was a few miles away from the café. Fishing was his favorite pastime and hobby. We both enjoyed each other's company there. On many occasions, I joined him not to fish but to spend quality time with him.

"Accountability, Chris means that you have direction in your life, and you can go it alone regardless of who is or is not in your life. But you also celebrate and are grateful whenever you have help from others. The thing is you must learn—never to lean on anyone. NEVER! At times being alone and yet not alone. Do you understand?" I nodded.

"Think about it I fish solo. And you, son, keep me company. So, the day you are out of town or sick, I still come here and fish. That is disciplining me to do what I love and to be accountable for my actions. In other words, I cannot control you. So, when someone chooses to leave you, it's far more than a choice. It's a decision. What you do with you is called accountability. To get that part of your life together, you need a job." Uncle Joe was determined to guide me. He offered me a part—time job at his café. I accepted his offer. Money was not an issue, but he insisted on paying me. I gave in.

Grandma Isabel and Izzy were delighted to learn that I would be joining them at the café in a few days. And yes, as an employee. Awkward···how was I going to act around Izzy?

CHAPTER TWO

Broken Pieces

It was a chilly day in Luce; a little cloudy too. Weather is appropriate for a jacket and cap, but I always wore that anyway. No changes were needed. I headed to the café, the only place that kept my sanity from repetitive thoughts I had about Amanda. Her residue lingered. Whenever she crossed my mind, it was like PTSD; I panicked. I felt anxious and restless. Those feelings of emptiness and loneliness were not as strong as they once were. I must admit, though, with time, things had gotten somewhat better. I could manage a day without falling apart. I kept busy.

Once at the Shop, I took my cap and gloves off. Besides being chilly, it was a great morning. Beams of light split through the windows from the sun peering between clouds. The café engine, which had gained full-steam, rumbled as Ms. Amber got to clean dishes, Eugene and Robert delivered fresh coffee beans, and Steve mopped the floor. I got right to the back where Izzy was. Everyone was busy. I joined in. We all knew about the morning humdrum. It was nicknamed 'humdrum' to signify a work—ethic like an assembly line. Everyone had to do their part to make the final product perfect. We literally assembled food and drinks. We worked like robots.

I refilled napkin dispensers, salt, and sugar packet holders. I zoned out the small talk and kept busy enjoying my work space. This routine gave me peace. Occasionally, a flash of Amanda's beautiful face crossed my mind as I swabbed the tabletops. I could see her alluring hazel eyes, long eyelashes, and those freckled dimples gracing her cheeks. I kept wondering why I wasn't enough for her. My ego had not let that part of my doubts go. Rejection may be the only thing humans hide from obvious expressions but deep down erodes our souls. I couldn't help but think about what she could've been doing and who was making her smile. I had given her everything, my—all. Those happy thoughts I once had slowly vanquished to sadness crowned with resentment. The Amanda I once loved deeply became the object of my hate. An enemy I hated, a monster, and a nightmare of my lifetime. I didn't want this negative vibe tracking my every being. My mind could only focus on the things she did wrong. I couldn't grasp how she used me and others as well. Equally confusing were her complaints about what others owed her and nothing about what she did for them. I could hardly think of any act of kindness except what Amanda felt entitled to. Could it be true when they say, "*There is a thin—line between love and hate?*" This relationship had hated trending all over it. Her departure released some type of sadistic aura around my life.

My happiness evaporated. It made no sense how I could feel so much affection for her and yet be devoid of the same feelings for me. This was a rude awakening because my feelings for Amanda were never mutual. They Felt cheated and maybe was in love with the idea of being in love. Anger and resentment had piled up inside. It was a pang of pain in my chest whenever I thought about her; she made me sick to my stomach. Maybe I hated being embarrassed, humiliated, or rejected.

How come I took for her like that? What was so special about Amanda? My ego had been crushed. And I hated it when people inquired about us. I grew tired of telling them she traveled and will be back soon. Her parents knew she had run away and kept it on the law while they privately searched. The last time I spoke with them, they admitted to seeing it coming. However, I was bothered by their reluctance to launch a public search for Amanda. Did they know where she was? My intuition was convinced that they had contacted her. At the minimum, they must have known her whereabouts. They, too, seemed distant from me, and with time, our communication came to a halt. In my mind, I saw this whole thing as a covert operation. I was on my own now.

Izzy snatched me out of thought when she rounded her hand on my bicep to place a menu at the center of the table. I got a whiff of her familiar scent as she slid by. I had known Izzy just as long as I had been with Amanda. Equally surprising was that I knew so little about her all these years. Noticing her demeanor and character commanded my admiration. I could relate more to Izzy than I did to Amanda. It wasn't a sexual attraction, even though I wanted that with her. It's just that she had more to give. Like me, Izzy hesitated to say what was on her mind and avoided direct confrontations with people. I discovered that quality in her whenever I visited Uncle Joe. We both loved to work and stayed busy. Even at home, Izzy enjoyed working on the project. It ranged from a simple drawing to journaling. She drew while the family conversed around the dinner table, hardly saying a word unless spoken to. I admired that about her. Conversations made me uncomfortable. It was a necessary evil. I didn't mind talking, just hated long conversations that left me feeling trapped. Uncle Joe was so good at that. When he talked with you, it didn't take long before you felt trapped. His line of questioning left you vulnerable and feeling like any answer you gave was too personal for comfort.

Izzy was much shorter than Amanda in stature. Her hair was plaited most of the time. She wore minimal makeup and appeared more of a naturalist. Her clothes fit firmly, revealing her sensuality. Her feminine traits were ever-present. I loved seeing her in jeans. They were always conservative and matched her body type. Her curvatures had fat and muscles in the right places. Her simple choices of sneakers were perfect for her age and style. A free spirit and invitation.

In contrast to Amanda, who revealed everything to the world, Izzy let her body speak for her. I wondered who she dated or considered dating. That side of her life remained mysterious and private.

We had a mutual admiration from a distance and hadn't conjured the guts to break the ice. Amanda and Izzy were equally beautiful, but Izzy and I never got that chance. I so badly wanted us to be more than friends. With Amanda gone, all I needed to do was take my chances. Ask Izzy for a date.

The hurdle was possibly convincing her that the drama she had seen between Amanda and me was not a reflection of my character. And that we were done. But again, Izzy must have heard Uncle Joe and aunty Madelyn come to my defense at some point. The stakes were too high. I doubted if the time was ripe to make my move on Izzy. Would Izzy think that she was the rebound or played second fiddle? I kicked myself for having dated Amanda. I may have lost a lot of good opportunities and a clear stab at a meaningful relationship.

"How was your morning?" Izzy asked me to stand by one of the island counters near the restaurant's center.

"It was fine; how about yours?" I peeked up at her.

She shrugged, "It was fine."

Izzy had thick eyebrows and pouty lips that gave her that infamous, innocent—look. She tucked a lock of hair behind her ear. I turned back to my own table and continued to clean. I enjoyed that Izzy and I had got to known each other without being very close. Of course, I frequented the café only as a guest and family member. At the back of my mind, I knew Uncle Joe must have said something around Izzy concerning my plight with Amanda. I could tell by the heightened empathy I received from her. Almost like she knew I needed my emotions nursed to healing. Or maybe she saw an opportunity for herself, too, not sure. But again, Izzy was tough to read. I couldn't tell if she liked me as a suitable mate or a step-God-brother.

My confidence about the possibility we could end up coupling was evident during my last training session. Ironically, Brad had come to the pool, too, with some girls to hang out. At first sight, I was shocked by how much weight he had lost. And secondly, I was equally surprised that he had not joined college. The guy did not need good grades to do it. Being a basketball star is always a guarantee of a free-ride scholarship. Shortly after his breakup with Amanda, Brad discovered I had taken over. One day he came over to the table where Amanda and I sat; full of ego; he reached over and tried to kiss her. I was in no capacity to physically challenge him to a fight. That incident hurt and was very embarrassing. I promised to start working out and bulk up to fight bullies like him.

Amanda was still reeling from their painful breakup and the humiliation she encountered at the mercy of Lori. In retaliation, she pushed his face up and out away from hers. "Good Job, girl!" I said quietly on the inside. She stood her ground. I also felt terrible that I couldn't fight him, even though I had been in fights with kids my own size in school before. This made me feel less than a man. I wanted so badly to strike him back for that.

As fate would have it, some things are just divinely orchestrated. Here I found myself near the archrival who ruined Amanda forever or, so I thought. He did not look like he did in High School. My looks were great in comparison. I had cut my hair and dyed it a lighter shade of blonde. The last time I saw my face, my cheeks had a massive show of power that dropped down to the jaw line. I have gotten rid of my binocular glasses and wore eye contact instead. I was ripped. There was no semblance of the geek—kid my former school mates could recognize.

So, Brad and the company created a scene, making noise and disturbances. Well, two teenage lads are lying on their towels drying up. I say so because I had seen them swim earlier. Brad pulled one of the kid's towels away from him. And I saw him beg for it back in vain. Brad kept tangling the towel higher, making the poor kid jump to snatch it back. To me, that was bullying 101. For some reason, I snapped. I saw my wimpy self in that kid being bullied. That, combined with the disrespect I had been dished on by Brad in Amanda's presence, called for blood. I dashed forward and told him to give the kid his towel back.

"We are just playing, dude chill." He told me as I approached him, seething with anger. He never saw it coming.

"Wham!!!"

"Wham!!!"

"Get—off me!" Brad was on the floor. I have no memory of what happened except for the flashes of pulling the towel from him, leaning forward, and connecting an upper cut right under his chin. The next moment, I found myself being held by my coach and two guys I don't know to this day. Brad's mouth was bloody.

"You're the geek from school. This is not over!" he yelled, admittedly defeated.

“Yeah, its not···remember Amanda···I’ll beat your···” I tried to set myself lose again from the army of claws that twisted around my waist, forming a chain lock. Brad was lucky that day—any day. As long as we never met.

“Chris, let it go. He’s not worth it. Enough! Enough!” My coach pleaded, clearly losing his grip on me.

“Okay, okay! I’m good···.”

“Are you sure?” He asked.

“I’m good—coach.”

I reached out to the kid and scrubbed his head as he smiled. It felt great. Finally, I had settled that score. But was not done with him···

Little did I know I was trending on social media. The fight video had been recorded and went viral among former schoolmates. Title;

"Brad's …. kicked by Chris, the Geek…" won't you know it, my mom called me about it within the hour. Uncle Joe had heard about the fight from Izzy too. He was furious that I fought Brad but glad I kicked his tail. I apologized profusely for it. My fear was dad finding out I was in a fight and from social media of all the places.

Well…well…well, somehow, I got word Amanda saw it too. She was impressed by my new physique. Apparently, she called me her "man" go figure. That was the text her mother had garnered the guts to forward. And with a smiley emoji like I needed an update on Amanda. They had avoided me all this time. So why the sudden change of heart? An enemy of my enemy is my friend, but that did not apply in this situation. Didn't need their cheerleading. It was too late for that. My concern was about dad and Izzy's reactions, nothing more. Somehow, I found myself caring for Izzy's feelings and thoughts. She teased me about it and with sarcasm that I had finally defended Amanda's honor and that it was a shame she wasn't there. I fired back and told her I did it for her and not my Ex. We laughed about it.

***

I snapped out of memory land to a symphony of smells and an orchestra of noises in the café. The aroma tranced my mind to hunger for fresh pastries from the oven, a zing of tropical-inspired dishes, and the good—old honey-baked ham. Uncle Joe was a quiet and calculating character of a man. And it showed in the café by the painting of the walls, a rich orange color, with accents of green and red—yellow. Our cooks conversed, standing by the sizzling pops of beef burgers over the grill as fragrant seasonings ascended from the stoves. Ms. Amber, as we called her, giggled over the cook's jokes as she kneaded dough over the swab counters. Waiters delivered hot meals to the tables and returned used dishes for cleaning. The system worked so well and kept us busy to think of anything else. Every element, down to the clanking of the dishes and the chatter of customers, carried away the bulk of my stress. Was I becoming a workaholic? Here, I found myself distracted, and that's exactly how I wanted it to be. Distraction from my pain—Amanda.

I dropped my rag and followed Uncle Joe when he signaled me to his office. I met Izzy, already seated and waiting for us. I made myself comfortable beside her on the wooden desk with our backs against the walls. Literally.

The café's commotion slowly faded behind us. His private office had a strong air freshener, which made my nose hurt. He was very particular about scents to the extremes, in my opinion. Izzy had difficulty breathing too. Our eyes caught each other at the corner, and her expression said it all. I smiled back.

"Your aunty and I are going to take care of some business. Izzy, you know where everything is located. Chris, watch over the place and help Izzy. Okay?" He sounded like a drill sergeant.

"How long?" Izzy asked.

"Not very long··· a few hours."

I sensed irritation by his reply, but I was up for the challenge, “Alright, no problem.” I said.

They headed out and left us in charge. I had no idea where to start but I couldn’t let Izzy down. Things went well. She got the cash registers, called in orders, and I handled the kitchen. I kept busy making sure cooks and waiters were moving. I didn’t particularly pay attention to what they did as much as ensuring movement happened. I cast my die on the idea that what needed to be done was done. And if they were busy, then work was done.

As cheesy as it is to admit it, we really were family. The sight of our coordinated efforts and smooth running of the café was undoubtedly rewarding. I didn't have much family; neither of my parents had siblings. We were possibly the loneliest nuclear family in the city. Wealth had its own downside. A school kid once told me, "The rich also cry."

The sunlight crashed and rolled in with heat like a tidal wave before settling the score to the west. We were busy. Hardly noticing Uncle Joe's loud absence. It was not until closing time that we realized they had not returned. Our minds were fixated on ensuring we didn't let them down, at least from my vintage point of view. I didn't ask Izzy if this had happened before, and she never cared to fill me in on the scoop either.

Closing the café wasn't hard, just inconvenient pain. Our bodies were worn out from the day's work. I was so ready to rest. The place had quieted down except for a few noises outside. This was it. A whole day of hard work. Izzy and I sat down to catch a break. We dimmed the lighting. Waited for Uncle Joe in silence. Izzy chose to sit by the mural of Hawaii. I joined her and sat on the other side of the booth. She took off her apron and made herself comfortable. Her face was oily. I thought it was cute, a hardworking—woman.

"You tired?" I asked with a half— smile.

"Really, Chris···" she rolled her eyes. Looked at the walls momentarily before sipping her Sprite.

I smiled and played it off. Gazed through the window and noticed the skies, partly blanketed by dark clouds. Soon to be overtaken by the imminent darkness of the night. I watched a strike of lighting map through them. A storm was on the way later that night. We kept the café temperatures cool, whether closed or open for business. The air conditioning kept humming as we patiently waited. I couldn't help but think about the cost of running a business. I wondered how much Uncle Joe lost in running costs.

"Can you call him?" I asked Izzy. She looked up and back down. Lazily rose and walked to the counter. I knew she was tired, but I did not want to be the one to call him. I heard the phone ring several times before it went to voice mail. She called two more times.

"That's okay. Maybe they are in a bad reception area." I said to myself. Izzy returned to her spot defeated. She dropped down without a care. She was tired.

"We give them fifteen minutes tops. Then we go. Do you know how to turn the alarm system on?" I inquired.

"What do you think?" She was out of it. Maybe it was her way of letting me know this had happened before. But it also confirmed she knew how to set the alarm. At this moment, I realized that I had come a long way in understanding women's emotions. I could tell the "leave me alone" signals. I backed off the pressure and sat there reading the menu like it was my turn to order. Needed to pass—the time.

After fifteen minutes and no sign of uncle Joe, I decided we were leaving. I stood up.

"Okay, it's time to go. I'll drop you off." I was confident. It was my turn to shine. She followed suit. I waited outside as she set the alarm ON and locked the door.

"Already then..." I said, grabbing both our aprons and hanged them on my back. Izzy complied and shuffled behind me to the car.

I've been to uncle Joe's house many times so getting there was not an issue. I took a turn into the city park instead. The thought of never trying to know Izzy outside of family kept nagging; wasn't this a golden opportunity? Whether she was tired, I was no longer playing the nice guy. The future was in my hands. And wanted her in it. I had to start somewhere, and this was that—where.

The huge lush green park wasn't far from the café. Two rights and a left, and bam! the artificial oasis rose into our field of view. I found a parking spot easily, and few people were there at that time of the night. The exception being a few natured—remnants taking in fresh scents of the pine. And I mean people and squirrels. Obviously, it was about to rain in a few moments. No bike riders, dog walkers, and other domestics lingered around. The parking location was close to the woodsy sidewalk. Izzy gave me the—look.

"What? I thought we should hang out a little, take a stroll and then go home." I confidently told her my plans, not needing her input on the matter.

Her eyes widened, and she nodded slightly in agreement at my sudden gesture. I felt great at her ability to go with the flow. This is what I had longed for from Amanda. A woman that would allow me to lead. Not all the time but some of the time. I cared about her opinions. If she had told me that she didn't want to go to the park, I would've not taken her by force.

That's the way I thought relationships should be. One suggested the other gave a benefit of the doubt or an alternative view and, at times, went along without reservations if the idea was good, to begin with.

"Are you sure? We don't have to."

"I want to," she said as I opened the car door and stepped out into the humid—air.

A slight breeze rustled tree tops as the storm front inched closer across the sky. The girl was tired and yet willing to stroll. I admired her shapely self, and watched her feet drop out of the car. I admired her even—more. Not because she was compliant but because she also felt something for me. She could not accept that offer unless there was more for me, she hadn't expressed.

"We'll not be going too far. It's almost raining." I assured her.

"Alright." She agreed, and we walked to the wooden bench closer to the first trail into the woods. Her hair was slightly tousled by the wind. Traffic sounds were faint in the distant. Here we had a beautiful scenic view of the park. I wondered if people took time out of their schedules. Tax dollars may be spent to a million, not counting maintenance costs. All in the name of conserving nature and providing a place for residents to enjoy. But in reality, no one seemed to care for the amenity. A silence befell our unity as we both swam—away in thoughts. I didn't know where to start or what to say.

That is not a good sign. I fidgeted and crossed my arms into my jacket. Why did I think this was a good idea, to begin with? When I glanced over, Izzy was calm and collected. She had lost herself in considering how expansive the park was and soaked it in silence. I thought women had it easy. They waited for the men to make a move. Their only action was to accept or reject the offer based on their moods, a list of choices, and how good a man's approach was. Did women ever think that the field of good men had shrank? Or that the good ones were taken? Where did they get this confidence that a good man would always come by if they lost the one in their sight? Those were universal questions above my thinking abilities. I only had one mission on my mind, and that was to conquer Izzy's heart.

"How is your photography coming, Chris?" she asked amid a wind gust that blew her hair into her face.

"Oh yeah, great... My camera is in the car right now." While saying that, I got up to get it. Partly because I wanted to show it off but mostly to gather my thoughts for the next move. I wanted this girl—Izzy. I hastily jogged to the car and back to her with a DSLR in my hand and switched it on.

"Looks nice." she said, nodding towards it in my hands.

"Thank you." I brought my camera to my eye level and adjusted the lens to focus. She was gorgeous through the lens.

"Hey, what are you doing?" She covered her face and chuckled. "Don't cover your face." I moved her hand. She stayed still long—

enough for the shutter to click and I reviewed the picture. "It's good." I leaned over to show her.

"No way you got a good picture in one shot?" She rolled her eyes. "I took a burst, so there's more than one. And I think you look amazing." She stared at herself on the camera screen.

"It's not all that great and was taken by force, so you should delete them."

"Well, I don't have any pictures of you, and since you are so camera shy, it was the only way." I smiled and sat next to her again. She and I looked forward in silence. I toyed with buttons on my camera as she kicked a few loose rocks across the park's trail. She looked at me and opened her mouth, but when I looked back at her, she remained silent and bit her lip. I sighed and adjusted my sitting posture. This was beyond awkward. It was downright painful! Didn't we know each other enough for small talk? I reasoned.

"Let's walk down the trail." I stood up. She hesitated and looked at the sky.

"Are you sure? It looks like pouring down any minute." I shrugged, "It might not. Besides, we'll be quick." I nudged her off the bench. She slowly stood up and put her hands in her jacket. We strolled together like an old couple with no particular place to go. The humidity made the air tangible. I could feel dense.

"So··· I never asked what college you attend?" My camera bounced against my chest as it hung around my neck.

"Still undecided. I dropped out of public school. I completed my High School online. I may join a private college soon." Izzy kicked a few small rocks with her feet playfully. I noticed her discomfort with the question. She continued, "I hardly have time after work."

"I thought you only worked at the cafe?" I turned to her as I spoke. "Yeah, that's where I work *full-time*!" She said.

"You work that much? That you can't fit school in between?" I asked.

"Not with the odd jobs they make me do. I fill in everything—missing. When someone calls in sick, I take on their workload as well. I clean the mess after everyone leaves. I train new hires and get blamed when things fall apart." Izzy was sad. This was not self-loathing over worked or underpaid. It could only be one or the other, not both. I was dumb, founded on the idea that uncle Joe could be inconsiderate of Izzy. Unless she was making this up.

I walked backwards to face her as she spoke for a moment. She seemed a bit frustrated. It felt like this was the first time she was opening-up. “I guess the job description is different for relatives, huh!” she concluded. I felt sad.

“I think uncle Joe has a plan for you. Somehow, it will pay off at some point.” Tried to end the trajectory this conversation had taken. We were not getting romantic. Instead, we were headed to the usual platonic zone. I was determined to change that. She was going to be my girl friend, my lover. Izzy would know that I’ve feelings for her.

I also learned that evening she lived with her grandmother Isabel. When I visited uncle Joe, I thought she stayed with them. Thank goodness if she did, Izzy would probably never get a break. Which was ridiculous considering how much of her life she had already given them at the café. New revelations about Izzy's life came out in a very short time. I couldn't wrap my head around it. All this time, I thought she lived with them. And now, she was finding out that she lived with grandma Isabel. Of course, I knew grandma was up there in age but I did not put two and two together. In addition, Izzy was related to uncle Joe and not Aunty Madelyn by blood. How come they decided she should live with Madelyn's mother? So just how much did I not know about them?

I knew they loved Izzy, but I don't think they understood her desires either. No wonder she kept to herself most of the time. And I thought she was quiet or, worst had temperament issues. Could it be that they just didn't see her ambitions beyond their family business? I was bothered.

"Well, what will you study for when you go back to school. Or if you're going back, I guess." I asked.

"Journalism." she shrugged.

"What? Do you like journalism? I never knew that." I bumped her shoulder with my own as we walked. We were getting deep into the trail. Thunder rumbled. She was startled. I reached over and held her hand.

"I'm not all that interested in it, honestly." she smiled awkwardly. She pulled the other hand into the sleeve of her jacket.

"But it's something I could see myself doing, and you can find work practically anywhere."

I stopped in my tracks as she spoke. Not letting her hand—go.

"You sure have a sacrificial outlook on life. Do you ever plan on enjoying yourself? Or doing something you love?" I inquired.

"I do··· I will. I just." she paused and pressed her lips together.

I raised my eyebrows at her and waited for an answer. She scoffed, "You don't even know the things I'm interested in! Why are you lecturing me about enjoying myself!" she rolled her neck as she spoke, and I laughed.

"Tell me you still draw—at least···." Her eyes seemed to twinkle at the fact that I remembered that. I mentally patted myself on the back. I had not seen her pleased like that.

"Yeah, I still draw when I get the time, of course." She smiled.

A chilly breeze went by, sending shivers up my spine. "I'll have to see some of your art soon." I tugged my jacket against the cold a little tighter.

She gave me a bashful expression, "I don't know··· I guess you will."

She looked me deeply in the eyes for the first time. I stopped walking and paused in front of her while she walked a few steps closer and stopped too. Izzy was shorter than Amanda, but both were not that shorter than me, so I didn't have to cram my neck downward when I looked at her. Rain drops cut our stare—short. A trickle of beads began crashing down, followed by a soft—roll of thunder. The storm had blossomed in the skies. A jolt of lightening and deafening thunder roared. We ran to the car. I let her lead the way. As we neared the car, I overtook her, opened her door quickly, and she jumped in. I ran around the car to the driver's side, opened the door, and slid in as fast as possible. We were getting soaked by the second. On the back of my seat was a towel I always kept. Was glad it was clean. Reached over, grabbed it, and handed it to her. She smiled···

We drove up and out of the park amidst a gust of wind that swung against us. Izzy squealed at the storm's violence as the water rolled with tapping sounds against the window.

It wasn't unusual for this kind of weather—trait in Luce. Storms passed through unpredictably. I kept the windshield wipers at full speed, and even with that, I could hardly see anything.

"Let's give the rain a few minutes. Maybe it'll pass." Izzy was nervous. The patter of rain on the rooftop made it hard to talk except shout at max—voice. To avoid straining my vision, I defogged the windows, kept my eyes on the road, and stayed calm throughout, and soon the rain stopped. Roads were wet and slippery. Drains could not handle the massive, makeshift rivers that threatened to sweep cars away. I had to be careful.

"It looks like the storm is clearing up," I assured her. But then we heard tornado sirens. The worst was behind us. Luckily my house was a couple of miles down from where we were. I decided to go to my place without telling Izzy anything. I didn't want to put our lives in danger initially. I had to make a quick decision intuitively without her input.

As I pulled into my driveway, Izzy was curious but understood we were under a tornado watch. Unbuckled my belt and signaled she does the same. We got out of the car and hurried to the house. She followed me. It was her first time coming to my place. This was not how I had envisioned her first visit. But here we were.

"I'll drive you home when the storm clears up."

"You can leave your shoes here." I pointed to nowhere in particular. She took off her shoes and met me in the kitchen, propping herself on the stool by the counter in front of me. The house was somewhat clean, and I didn't have to worry about her thinking I was a slob. Yet I fidgeted with random things around the kitchen to seem like I was looking for something when I was just nervous.

"A drink, juice, anything?" I opened the cabinet to feed her.

"Um, not really. No," she replied and spun her hips back and forth. Suddenly rain started chucking down outside. A ripple of thunder sounded, making Izzy glance through the window and then back at me, a bit worried.

"So, when do you think the storm will die down?" She asked. I shrugged while trying to think of what we could do in the meantime.

"No worries let's watch television until it does," I suggested nodding her over to the couch. She followed me to the living room and sat together on the sofa. My living room was muted with shades of cream; tall shadows climbed the walls, a reflection of the dimmed lamps in the corners. It was awfully quiet until I put on a random thriller, I had from my movie collection. I glanced over to read her expression once the movie started needing to gauge her level of interest. She seemed a bit··· blank. I cleared my throat to fill the silence, and she glanced over to me and back to the lit screen. I wanted to say something but thought it best to let the moment flow.

"So, when was the last time you visited Hawaii?" I asked.

"I haven't," she adjusted herself on the couch at the sudden spark of conversation. "I haven't been back there since I was born. But

I plan too. I don't remember much about it, but still connected, you know." she said, staring at the television.

I understood what she meant. The condo I lived in had been in the family since childhood. When my dad bought the big—house, things turned for the worse. I thought mom was going to be happy with the new place. She complained serially about the condo is too small. At one point, she told dad that he needed to do more like uncle Joe and aunty Madelyn. For they had bought a house before we did. She felt like the condo was more of an apartment and wanted more space and room. Mom did not like close living quarters. Well, we had it all a big—house, and land spread in the backyard too. So, what else was left undone?

Whatever this was, it had taken a toll on my family. We had gone three separate ways. My dad was out there somewhere, mom in our mansion, and I was the youngest bachelor in town to have lived in an upscale condo. At first, dad worked many hours buying and selling homes to make ends meet. Long work hours turned into days away from home, and soon, it became the norm for him not to be around. He kept the condo and never sold it. My mom started her own business ventures to keep me busy. It felt like a silent competition and a proxy war. Their inherent frustrations turned into competition without a word about it. In a way, mom was competing with dad. I had become the middle ground. When advantageous, she blamed him for not being there for me. The easiest way to strike back for missing him was to use me instead. She did not want to ask him to stay longer on vacations or spend time with her. Maybe ego had something to do with it. Not wanting to be a party to the feud, I threatened to run away. The consolation price was that I moved into the condo. Finally, I had some peace. Truth is, I loved both equally. Could not blame either one of them for the turmoil. I gave up on the possibility of reconciliation and, instead, went with the flow.

"Yeah, I do. I'm connected to this place, you know? It's where I grew up. Even though we've had some rough times, there are many good memories also." Izzy and I settled in for the movie.

"So, just out of curiosity, are you Polynesian?" I asked.

She shook her head, "My mom is Polynesian, and my dad is African-American. I have a lot of family in Hawaii on my mom's side."

I chuckled, "You hardly talk about your mother. How is she?" At that moment, Izzy had a troubled look on her face. Had I crossed the line?

"You don't have to answer. If I crossed the line." I hurriedly added.

"She's not here," Izzy answered without moving her eyes from the TV screen. We were finally having a normal conversation before my foot got into my mouth. This was not the time to bring sensitive issues. I hated myself for getting too—greedy.

"She passed away? I'm sorry; I didn't know. No one told me. I shouldn't have asked." Her eyes perked up at me as she laughed under her breath.

"No, I meant she isn't here in Luce." She replied. I let out a staggered sigh.

"Yeah, she's in Florida with her sister and one of my aunts. They take care of her because..." she hesitated and then continued, "Mom has a mental illness. It flared up badly while pregnant with me, and that's why my parents are separated." It was hard for her to say that.

I couldn't believe Izzy went through so much. I mean, her dad was in the military, and that's why she stayed with her grandmother, but this whole thing about her mom was new to me. I had so many questions, and it was refreshing that she had opened up to me about them.

"So, how much of your family lives in Hawaii?" I asked while adjusting myself to face her more.

"Lanai. Others on the mainland." She answered.

I nodded. Uncle Joe had mentioned it before. I knew there was some bad—blood in the family but did not know to what extent. Her family must have had some challenges too.

"Your family is so much more interesting than mine. You have an extended family and all that. My grandparents are dead except one. I'm an only child, funny, huh?" I sighed. It sounded whiny coming out of my mouth.

She smiled at me.

"But you're a genius, and so are your dad and grandfather." She said, referring to me being a third-generation Holmes inherent.

"Your whole family is self-employed, and you have so much under your name. Besides, bright people tend to be independent, so it's not weird that you live on your own" I couldn't help but smile as she comforted me. "And let's not forget you're the highest-ranked swimmer in the state" she nudged my bicep, and I laughed.

"Yeah, I guess that's true, but it can be lonely without having a family," I said, and she nodded in agreement.

"Izzy, do you have a boyfriend?" I blurted out. To be honest, mastery of the mouth was my weakest link. When I needed to know something, I just put it out there. "Where did that come from?" Her eyes widened.

"Well, you know···Izzy, you are beautiful and intelligent. I just cannot see how you have not been snatched. I guess they are not handsome enough···or scared of beauty."

"Not since Tony." she teased, and a flame of jealousy—anger sparked in me.

I had known Tony for a long time. I recalled Tony flirting with her. At the time, my eyes were on Amanda. Hardly realized Tony and Izzy had taken it to a new level. How much had I missed while coupled with Amanda? I thought Tony was mischievous when he told me they had a movie date. I never cared for the scoop; I was just happy they did. Back then, it didn't bother me. Somehow, when she told me that they dated, a lace of jealousy rose in me.

"You seriously haven't dated since Tony?" she shook her head.

"No, I haven't."

"Well, why not?"

"No one worth—dating."

"That's harsh."

"And Tony was worth dating? I mean, you know···just curious···you liked the twirl in his hair?" I asked as my finger took one of her curly hair—locks and twirled it around.

She pushed my hand away and laughed with embarrassment. "We were teenagers. " she shouted and hid her face behind the couch pillow she had clutched.

"Oh! I remember that's why he called you Ms. Dawson···." I teased.

"Well, you weren't any—better with Amanda," she said. I chuckled and glanced at my lap. She was right, but the thought of Amanda seemed to suck authenticity out of my jealousy. Izzy noticed it immediately. I think she enjoyed my attraction to her.

"What if that actually happened? Tony and I, you and Amanda." She asked.

"That would've been ideal in our teenage years," I chuckled··· "But as adults, never···." At my response, I realized Amanda was finally dead in my heart. I had gotten over her. Izzy picked up on it.

"Mediocre relationships are 50/50, but real relationships are 100. You'll find someone worth giving your 100 to, Chris."

I looked at her in a surprised way. "Did you pick that up out of a tacky relationship advice book?"

"No, the last time I saw my dad, I asked him why he didn't leave my mom even though she was losing her mind, and that's what he told me. That she was worth 100 percent of his love. And as far as I know, he's not getting remarried. He still hasn't even divorced her. I mean, they're separated but not divorced." She hugged the couch pillow. "I guess that's also why I haven't dated. I want to be with someone I can't live without." she was reflective.

I didn't respond; I just kind of nodded and took in what she had said. I wished my parents could've seen life through the same lens. I knew my mom discouraged recreational dating but was she earnest about loving my dad? As far as I remember, my dad appeared to look for ways to make mom happy, but she kept moving the goalpost. He just gave up. Maybe I was biased being a man, but the truth existed there. I'm sure some of it was subliminal angst, but my psyche was always on point. An explosion blasted from the movie scene and snapped me out of my thoughts and back to the screen.

After the movie ended, we put on another one. Izzy had gotten comfortable. To be honest, I enjoyed her company. The condo finally came back to life. It had been months since anyone other than my temporary house help had come over. The storm calmed down somewhat, and Izzy had not asked about going home. So, I let the issue—slide. If she was not going to bring it up, I was not going to spoil the moment. We ate some snacks out of laziness and kept watching movies. She asked for a blanket. It had cooled off. I gave her one of my own from the spare bedroom. And she cozied herself in it···

***

My neck ached as I surfaced from my sleep. Slivers of sun rays beamed into the living room. I adjusted my crimped neck on the arm of the couch. Birds chirped outside. I quickly glanced at the clock on the wall. Equally surprising, it was around 6 a.m. in the morning. A surge of energy blasted my usual nap head away. Izzy was a baby—asleep. We were on the couch and had no idea how we fell asleep and for how long we slept. From the looks of it, we must have dozed off while the movies played. She resting peacefully on the opposite side of the couch. Her legs stretched across my lap, her head propped on the couch pillow. I watched as she gently breathed sound—asleep. I let that moment sink in. Her hair was messy and sprawled over her face. A sleepy face and a little swollen and puffy lips made her look childishly cute. Carefully, I moved her hair away from her face. This was a good sight and a much-needed change in my life. I wanted to be more than just friends.

My phone rang two times. I picked it up with an embarrassingly raspy morning voice. I glanced at the screen; it was aunty Madelyn. Oh, men! Trouble? Too late, the ringing had woken Izzy.

“Hello,”

“Hello···”

“Is this Chris?”

“Yep, Aunty.”

“How are you?”

“Good··listen, Joe and I want to speak with you this morning. It's important. Can you drive over?" My throat immediately went dry. Did they know Izzy spent at my house?

"Okay, aunty, I will be over there shortly. Is everything okay?" I inquired—nervously.

"Yes, everything is fine. We are on our way to the house. Meet us there." She seemed distraught but not upset.

"Will do. Bye, aunty." I ended the phone call. This time around, my words that seemed to fly out without thinking were nowhere to be found.

They weren't in town? I guess they must not have known that Izzy didn't come home either. Talk of the princess, she sat upright with panic written over her face.

"What's going on?" Izzy asked, grabbing my shoulders.

"They weren't in town yesterday, and they're just coming back now. They said we are meeting at their house, but I don't think they know you're not with grandma." I quickly lined up my alibi. It was raining last night, we were under a tornado watch, Izzy stayed at my house, and we did nothing wrong. The storm ended late, and we watched movies. Nothing between us happened. Wait a minute, we were adults, right?

"Grandma goes to bed before I come home from work, so if we leave now, we can make it home before she gets up," she said, scrambling off the couch.

"Okay, let's go," I said, running to my bedroom.

"No, wait, I need to shower really quick." She lamented, standing in the middle of the living room.

"Girl—you crazy!"

"I need to get you there before she wakes up. You just said it yourself." Irritated but more worried.

"I know, I know. I'll jump in and out, promise···" she begged.

"Uhm···okay. Quickly." I pointed to the bathroom across.

She ran to the bathroom and slammed the door behind her. Wow! I had no time to think about that. I skated across the wooden floor to the bedroom. I yanked, pulled up and off my T-shirt, and squeezed a clean one. Had no time to think.

"Chris! Chris!" Izzy screamed.

“What···” I screamed back, my head stuck in the T-shirt as I squeezed it through. I once appreciated being skinny at one point in my past life.

Skidded across the floor to the bathroom she was in. What a sight! Izzy’s head peeped through the door as she held it ajar.

“I need a towel and a washcloth quick! Hurry···” Her face was wet.

“Okay, coming right up.” Helter-skelter I went looking for the items and returned at the same speed. She smiled and shut the door behind her. The shower hissed at max pressure. “That must be one hot shower,” I thought to myself.

CHAPTER THREE

Home Sweet-Home

The part of Luce where Izzy and grandma Isabel lived was completely worn down. The property was unkept, windows boarded, cats roamed everywhere, a few stray—dogs, grass grew in dusty patches, and sidewalks were scattered with litter. No one had to even ask how safe the neighborhood was on that side of town. This was my first time driving there. I was not concerned about it, but I knew Izzy was. She looked shamed by the fact that I was going to see where she lived.

Thirty minutes was enough to get to uncle Joe's home from the café. I silently prayed that her grandma would not be up when we got there. That, and I needed to revise my alibi once again just in case she asked us prodding questions. Grandma lived quite ways from anyone of us. So, I needed the address and directions from Izzy. The fact that she had to catch a bus from grandma's house to the café for work infuriated me. After giving me the address, she remained silent as I drove. Didn't say much. From the looks of it, I must have been on the right path, for she didn't correct my directions nor comment on my aggressive driving—style. GPS knows everywhere, I thought.

"If they ask where you were last night, let me answer first, okay..." I told her.

"Why? Is there something wrong with my answer? I'm a big girl." She replied.

"Of course, you are. I'll tell them there was a tornado watch, and they could not drive you home last night. So, we crushed at my place." Tried to reassure me.

Honestly, it wasn't a big deal that she stayed over. Amanda and her friends had done it severally over the years. I didn't cross any lines. By that, I mean—sex. I wasn't sure about Izzy's family. Especially grandma Isabel. I just hoped that she would not get in trouble because of me. By the time we got there, the sun had risen into the skies, turning the morning into a beautiful, friendly shade of blue. It was adventurous driving so fast to a place I knew nothing about. Izzy stared through the window most of the way there. I hoped that her thoughts were good from the night before. It was our first day and night together and that was a bonus. A whole 24 hours with Izzy. As we pulled up in their driveway, Izzy was too comfortable to sit upright. She had leaned on the side of her seat and loosened her belt. She had the look of one coming home from a vacation. What a bummer! Her silence was much welcomed in my life. I hadn't been close to anyone who kept quiet and enjoyed my company in a long time. Our silence during the drive could be an asset in the long run. Her love for art and affinity for nature was the icing on the cake. We had a lot in common, with one exception, I wanted to be more than just friends. A gigantic maple tree spread in front of their yard. It was seriously—huge. A thousand years could fit an age perfectly for such a majestic creature of nature. How many storms, dry spells, wars, and days had this tree seen? I wondered. Then, I remembered it must have been the tree uncle Joe talked about, raking leaves all day. Finally,

I had been accorded the pleasure of seeing it in person.

Izzy darted towards the front door, and I stood by the tree in admiration of its massive—spread. Obviously, every moment counted on this mission. The worst blunder Izzy and I could make was to get caught doing nonsensical things like standing by the tree instead of rushing into the house before grandma woke up. When that reality sunk in, I cut short my appreciation for nature and dashed after Izzy.

She fumbled with the keys in her bag, pulled them out, and unlocked the door while avoiding unnecessary noises. But the door squeaked a little. She poked her head in, looked around, then proceeded to step out of the way and let me in. She pointed to the stairs ahead of us and signaled a green light for me to go ahead as she turned around and locked the door behind us. I was halfway up when Izzy zoomed by me. She was as light as a feather and swift as a mountain goat. Her speedy tiptoeing caused me to panic, and I chased after her. She waited for me at the top. I glanced back to make sure no one trailed us. Once in her room, we were safe. I jumped on her bed and star fished across her bed covers.

"Why were you running so fast? Did grandma see you?" I asked.

"No, I couldn't let you beat me up the staircase." She chuckled as if it was the most obvious thing. Izzy dropped her shoulder bag to the floor.

"Are you kidding me? I seriously thought we were about to get caught!"

She shrugged and giggled.

Her bedroom was covered in violet color and darkened wood. It was cozy and full of hefty old—lady antique furniture. A kingsize bed, several dressers, a mirror, and even a wardrobe. True to the old-school design, the carpets were thick and worn out. Her headboard was jammed with a huge collection of stuffed animals.

"Are these animals gifts?" I reached and grabbed one of them, a sea turtle. Looked like the Ninja—Turtles.

"Most of them are. I never throw my stuff away." She laughed.

"My suffices are cute. You like the Ninja?" She asked.

"Yeah," I replied, fumbling with the toy. It was squishy with purple eyes. I remembered the year Izzy dropped out of school. We were watching basketball when one of the girls said Izzy was not returning to school. I was surprised and wondered what had happened. I think it was Amanda who said that she had family issues. I quickly corrected her, "Amanda, Izzy is just fine. She will be back."

"And how do you know?" Amanda was irritated. As always, she questioned my sources.

"Uncle Joe had not mentioned anything like that, Amanda," I replied. I knew uncle Joe was a caring man, and there was no way he would let Izzy drop out of school like that. Amanda knew her family as well. And she may have just blurted out her own thoughts.

Amanda would say anything to stay at the center and or draw attention. Maybe other kids at school made her feel insecure; I didn't know. But to say Izzy dropped out of school because of family issues was a blatant lie. If anything, Amanda fit that profile too—well herself. Back then, guys often commented on Izzy's natural and beautiful looks. She didn't need makeup or fake hair. That, I'm sure, had gotten to Amanda and rubbed her the wrong way. She was anything but natural. We all knew it. But no one dared talk about it. She wore excessive makeup, short—short skirts, weaves, nail extensions, you name it, she wore it.

When I looked up, Izzy had already changed into a soft jersey, jogging pants, and panda—slippers. She was oddly comfortable in my presence and in her room. In a strangely good way, I liked her sense of calm. Her closet door remained open as she tidied up the small mess on the floor, hardly paying any attention to me. I could see the subtle differences between Amanda and Izzy. For example, Izzy was socially responsible and kept things organized. She wasn't too much into fashion. But whatever she wore would fit the occasion. Like the quick—shift from work clothes to house clothes.

"Do you realize we spend a whole day and night together?" Her tone was more like a statement than a question.

"No, really?" I got up, leaned on the door frame of the closet, and watched her.

"Get back on the bed. Silly!" she commanded. Mindfully tucking her outfit into the proper fold while fussing with her hair as it kept falling into her face.

"Yes, Mam. Laughed out loud. I splashed on the bed."

"Be careful." She warned, "Lady Isabel might hear you and think we are getting robbed."

I liked her game of words. she beckoned. I got up. So, I did. Izzy swooped the hair behind her ear; I pulled her into me by the hand and wrapped my arms around her. Her eyes grew twice the size of how closely I held her. She had gotten used to my unorthodox ways of doing things. But I couldn't help it, and I liked the moment. She was safe in my arms. Izzy stared into my eyes for what felt like an eternity. I was tempted to break eye contact from her long—gaze to regain control. But just before I did, she pushed me away.

“What are you doing!” she fumbled back a few steps.

“I just wanted to see how you would react” I shrugged and played it off.

Before I could mull over my fantasy, Izzy leaped forward towards me. She wore an embarrassed look; I felt a little puppy—sad but smugger than anything. Was it pompous for me to feel proud that I made her blush? I froze at the moment as she swung her arms around my neck, pulled herself up on her toes, and gently kissed my lips.

“You like that?” Searching my eyes.

“Yeah, I do⋯.”

“Does it mean⋯”

“Hey, don’t take it too far now.” She drew a boundary.

The door made a creaking sound. We both heightened. Grandma Isabel peeped through. Her eyeglasses were as foggy as ever. She avoided making it in all the way.

"I knew something was fishy." she rolled her eyes. I greeted her with a cheeky smile.

"Madelyn and Joe are here. Grandma went for it. They saw your car in the driveway and didn't know Chris was already in the house."

"Uh··· I let him in, grandma." Izzy spoke up.

She nodded in response to Izzy and then signaled us out. "Come on then. Let's see what this meeting is about." She disappeared into the hallway. Izzy's head immediately snapped towards me. Again, I smirked at her in a 'w*e didn't get caught'* sort of way. Smiling, she rolled her eyes.

Downstairs in the living room, the air was unusually tense. The expected mahogany—antique types of furniture were spread artfully and everywhere. Their house could easily qualify for a Smithsonian collection. Grandma sat in her rocking chair by the window. Uncle Joe made himself comfortable on the loveseat at the furthest corner of the room. Why was Uncle Joe and aunty Madelyn not cozying up? Did they fight on that trip? So far, I knew that they had just returned from wherever they went. Were they breaking up? Okay, there was no need for speculation, I told myself. The moment of truth was at hand. Madelyn, Izzy, and I sat on the crunched—sofa. There was silence···this wasn't good. Finally, after an eternity of squeaks and folds, uncle Joe spoke up.

“Well, I don't actually know how to say this. But it's been going on for some time now,” he cleared his throat. Okay, here we go! I thought to myself. I glanced around the room to catch reactions. Still, everyone seemed focused on what uncle Joe was about to say except aunty Madelyn. This was a breakup; I was sure of it. For starters, aunty had unnecessarily squeezed her big butt between Izzy and me. She knew we couldn’t fit comfortably. But chose to sit with us and not her husband.

“I’ll be closing down the café in a few days.” He breathed heavily into the words and looked away to avoid direct eye contact with us.

Izzy gasped and covered her mouth.

“What!!!” My thoughts came out as expected…

"We've tried hard to keep it, but it won't stay afloat. I thought she was going to make it, but everything tanked." He sounded apologetic. A defeated man always felt sorry for himself and those that counted on him next. Uncle Joe had given—up.

Glancing at Madelyn, I could tell she felt the lowest seeing her husband give up. But was it just the café or something else?

"This explains a lot, uncle Joe. Is that why you've been taking many trips out of town?" Izzy was visibly and understandably upset. I got my first clue. So, when they left that night, Izzy had been through it. No wonder she wasn't herself. She had invested time and energy. Her youth was almost gone helping them, and for what exactly? Seeing the end of it amounts to nothing more than losses and wasted time? This must have been a bitter pill to swallow. And rightly so. It didn't sit well with her. My heart went out to Izzy.

"The cafe has taken all the money. There's nothing left." Uncle Joe said.

Grandma had the radio on and country music played in the background and in a low tone. I wish we had an inspirational moment. This was like planning for a funeral.

"So, what are you gonna do? Are we job-hunting now? I mean...I can help you." A flicker of angry—emotions ran over my face. This was that time in my life I could've been helpful to them for all they had done for me. Besides, I wanted something out of this for Izzy too. I sincerely thought that uncle Joe was planning to hand over the café to Izzy when she came of age. They had no children of their own, and obviously, their strong affinity to Izzy and being their niece, working for them. All that counted for something, an inheritance, for crying out loud.

My parents had no problems, but I also knew whatever assets and businesses they accumulated were mine to inherit. That fact was not in contestation. I was already in one of my assets, the— condo. Closing the café meant Izzy was the biggest loser in all this. How were they going to afford her tuition? The café was her only stab at normality. My heart melted···

"We're moving··· to Florida." Uncle Joe replied, avoiding eye contact.

Wow! Florida! We froze like ice sickles. And now? Was aunty the only one prepared for this bombshell?

"Honey, we didn't talk about that." Madelyn was furious.

"I know, but that's what I've been thinking." He replied.

"Are you serious?" She tried to engage him. A little embarrassed that even she had been put on the spot without warning. Or maybe this was just a front to throw us off. Either way, we did not buy that crap, not even herself. Grandma sighed—loudly. That was a sign. If grandma didn't believe their fake disagreement, Izzy and I had no choice but to side with her.

"This is not just about you, Joe." She teared up.

"My family gave you the money to launch this café in the fast place. I have to think about how I will explain to them. And you want to cut and run?" She was shaking.

"Oh···crap Joe. Stop that." Grandma said in a low tone and rose from her chair.

"Madelyn, I raised you better than this. You side with Joe on everything in private and this, right here, is bull. And you know it." Adjusted her glasses and gave uncle Joe the—look.

"I'm too old to be moving from one place to another. Grow up! These young folks are looking up to you. Do you want them to cut and run every time they get a challenge?" She got emotional.

"My health isn't good to relocate. You all come back when I'm dead and bury me in the backyard. Not moving." Grandma was emotional.

"Mom, wait, don't leave. Please sit down for a moment." Aunty Madelyn pleaded.

"I need a break. Going to watch family feud. Grandma had heard enough of the chaos. It reminds me of this family."

My head stopped processing shortly after he said he would close the café in a few days. I needed some time to process it. I could not wrap my mind around it. Ever since knowing them, cracks opened in their perfected union for the first time. Was their family any different from mine? What about the man—talk uncle Joe had pushed me into believing?

"What?" My voice was agitated. I could feel everyone in the room getting tense. They all knew what I had been through. They were the only normal thing to me that resembled a family. I didn't care about the money. If money could get the issue resolved, I would be willing to help.

"Why are you moving to Florida? Why do you have to move in the first place? There are jobs and business opportunities here as well!" I felt my throat straining. Aunty Madelyn sighed in frustration on the couch while uncle Joe looked at the ground and got emotional. I leaned on him when my family wasn't there for me. The impact of his decision would easily be felt around the city. We had clients who could not go about their business without first stopping by the café for a fresh cup of coffee. And then their friends in the neighborhood. The list could easily run into thousands to be flatly ingenious about it. I had just lost Amanda and couldn't risk losing them too. This wasn't an option. Call me selfish, but I had to do something about it.

"Uncle listen, I can help. I will talk to dad even if I have to sell the condo to save the café." Putting it all on the line.

"Hey, Kid, I know you mean well. But you must understand. I don't need your father to bail me out. Neither would I consider your option to sell the condo. Business is no guarantee. If that was the case, I would've sold my house first to save the café." He said.

"Why didn't you sell the house? We could've moved in with mom." Madelyn chimed in and challenged Joe.

"Madelyn, not now! Just keep off."

"I'm sick of it all."

"This whole thing was a big mistake. I should've taken a job instead." Uncle Joe's voice grew louder and angrier.

"What about me?" Madelyn softened.

"What about you? Huh," He was visibly aggressive.

"I know I took your family's money. What do you think I feel like? Huh! A winner or a loser?" He stood up erratically and held his arms on his hips. Nothing about him was the usual calm and collected uncle Joe I knew.

"You just want to return to your family in Florida. GO!" She screamed and sobbed···loudly. I never mattered anyway.

"I have not been there for Tori and Rylan. You know Tori's mental health and all. They're struggling too. Madelyn, you are going with me or not?" Awkward···

"Leave my mom out of this⋯." Izzy broke her silence.

"No, honey, it's not that. Your uncle is just frustrated." Madelyn held Izzy as she broke down.

I'm family too, but I couldn't bring myself to say it. What would I look like? Was I more important than their blood relatives? Could they choose me over the rest of their family members? Maybe if they had adopted me, I would've counted. There was no reason for them to stay in Luce. I could feel my heart rate picking up. Panic attacks were not new to me. I felt one on the way—not good. I could deal with the moving thing later, but I couldn't let Izzy see me like this.

There was absolutely no way she was going to see me fall apart. I swore to myself. I very rudely got off the couch and stormed out of the house. No questions. Madelyn called after me while I headed out; she knew my history of anxiety attacks. She was my godmother, after all. Once it started, I had to be alone to catch my breath. I cranked my engine, hit the reverse gear, and pulled back and out of the driveway as fast as possible. On the periphery, I caught a glimpse of Izzy on the front porch. She helplessly folded her arms, looking at me as I drove away. Between splits of memory, I stared at her for a moment, then continued to drive. I could deal with her later. I knew she was distraught. These were tough times calling for tough measures.

***

I had been staring at the ceiling from my bed for a while. I hadn't eaten or moved at all.

My thoughts floated in the Milky—Way of the ceiling. The only noise I heard came from the constant buzzing of my cell phone. It was, of course, Madelyn, the third time calling. I was ashamed of the situation. I knew Madelyn understood what was happening with me, but not Izzy. The thought that she may have told her frightened me. I could not face her any more than the shame that ate at my soul. I reasoned that Izzy would not want to date a man with panic attacks. On her fourth call, and out of respect, I picked it up.

"I know you're upset, but hear me out, Chris. Your uncle··· Joseph... He's been going through so much; you don't even know the other—half. He's been dreading telling you this for so long. I know you have a right to be upset, but I'm begging you not to be. Just be here for us during this time···Okay?" She paused... "You had asked us what you could do to help. Being here for us would help a lot." She concluded. Her voice was hopeless—apologetic.

"I'm still upset··· but that doesn't mean I'm not going to be there for you guys. I will help with everything, but I think this is unfair." I replied, staring at the ceiling.

"I know it is."

"But I'm glad you're not backing out on us." Sounding relieved that I had opened it.

"Please come back."

"Not now, aunty, no disrespect. But I need alone time for now."

"Yep." I sighed.

"The place won't be shutting down in a few days. I'm hoping to keep it open more than your uncle does. I think aunty needed me just as much. I understand how you men think." She waited for my affirmation.

"I can help, I want to offer you some money to save the café, but I know uncle Joe would never accept it. I bet my dad has no idea his best friend needs his help. Am I right?" I asked···

"Of course, you are, Chris. Just think that he needs you around." she answered, tiptoeing around the question.

"Your uncle has too much pride to do something like that. You're coming to the café on Saturday, right? Please promise." She begged.

"Will do," I assured her.

“Oh! By the way, did something happen between you and Izzy yesterday?” My body froze at her question.

“Um··· No. why?”

“No big deal, it's just that she seemed really upset after you left. I mean, we all are, but it was more on Izzy. But you said nothing happened, so it's fine.” She concluded.

“If you must know, she’s a basket case. Not sure if it’s the café or you.” Aunty had a way of giving you a heads-up.

Once we got off the phone, I wondered what was different about Izzy that made her bring it up to me? I dropped my phone to the side, staring at the ceiling again. I had training sessions lined up the following morning. There was no way I could miss that. Being a Friday, I was going to complete my routines, rest for the evening and then go to the café on Saturday morning. But could I wait that long without seeing or speaking with Izzy? The thought of Izzy leaving Luce spawned a black hole in the pit of my stomach. I'd do anything for them not to leave.

***

The sun was shining, yet it was bone-chillingly cold. I caught a shiver in mid-conversation with uncle Joe. We were having a reconciliation, if you will. Fishing at the pond was our getaway place for the man—talk. We were free to hold a meaningful conversation there. As expected, uncle Joe expressed his remorse and how badly he felt about the situation. As a matter of fact, he had pulled me away from my morning shift at the café to talk things over. I had no choice but to oblige to his request. After all, he was the boss. The man was in troubled waters and needed a listening ear.

I would learn that day that he had been very accommodating to aunt Madelyn over the years. Without a child of their own, extended family members on both sides shamed them in secret. He had to suck it in and put on a brave face. Aunt Madelyn regretted that uncle Joe could get a child with any woman but chose not to break his marriage vows. He confided in me that aunty had an abortion at a very young age. She had gotten pregnant, and knowing that her family could've thrown her out literally, she begged her then-boyfriend to take her in. But he was no good. He was a party—animal, sold out to music and the nightlife. As fate would have it, she found out that he had also gotten another girl pregnant as well, and around the same time. How would he be a father to two children practically the same age? Not to mention that the other woman was willing to do bodily harm to Madelyn just to keep to herself. So, aunty chose to abort. Well, with one challenge. Her pregnancy wasn't showing just yet, so her parents had no idea. She was desperate, naïve, and had no money.

The to-be baby—father was unwilling to help her foot the bill either. Afraid and alone, Madelyn was confused. Even contemplated suicide. In a panic, she found the courage to disclose the issue to a close friend. She had recommended her to a lady who specialized in homeopathic remedies. To cut a long story short, things didn't go well. Aunty almost died.

The bleeding was so bad that what was meant to be a secret spilled into a medical emergency. Surgery had to be done. From uncle Joe's best knowledge, part of the fetus had remained in the womb, and that was very dangerous. Her life was at risk. Well, she had a hysterectomy to save her life. Aunty's parents were so disturbed and never fully recovered from it. One can only imagine the emotional trauma she endured at that age. So, when she fell in love with uncle Joe much later and in her twenties, her father gave her uncle the investment money for the café. Since that is all, he talked about. And, of course, uncle Joe took the money. He didn't come from a well-off family; any help to launch his dream was welcomed. In a way, Madelyn's parents were offloading a troubled child to uncle Joe without his knowledge.

He found out about the abortion and the surgery situation while married. What was he to do? Abandon her? No, he took on her burden. In sickness and in health, in wealth and in poverty. She had endured emotional pain, confusion, and depression. He became the father, friend, and husband, all that wrapped into one. He bit the bullet and told whoever wanted to know that he was the one who could not have a baby and not his wife. This is just how much uncle Joe loved his wife. As fate would have it, her father passed on, and grandma Isabel became a widow. Guess who took her in? Madelyn did; to make matters worse, grandma never asked for forgiveness; aunty Madelyn longed to hear.

Yes, she made a huge mistake. But she was young and experimenting. The tragedy of being barren and watching her husband be less than a man when she knew it was perfectly fine to sire a child ate at her core. That was the reason they stuck so close. It was them versus the world.

“Aren't you going to miss Luce?” I inquired.

“You mean the city? Yes, of course. We are at the center of it. Prime location and all.” He adjusted the worm on the hook···

“They are not biting today. When it's wrong, all go—wrong.” He lamented.

“Are you ready to leave?” I asked, looking at my hands.

“I don't think I’ll ever be ready, but it's what I have to do, you know?” Deep down, I knew he meant every word, but it sat bitterly in my stomach. He stared at the scenery on the horizon.

“You know our leaving doesn't mean you're not family anymore. Right?” He inquired about my truest emotions.

“I believe you, but it doesn't sit well.” I laughed, “I’m just so sick of being betrayed. I’m always the one left behind.” I whined.

“Well, especially with that attitude.” He said. I looked up at him, confused.

“How often do I have to tell you that people will treat you how you perceive yourself. What do you expect to attract if you always see yourself as the one left behind?” He went there. Real—talk.

“Is that why you’re leaving? Huh? Did I attract this situation too?” I waved my hands whimsically. "I'm sick of everyone not owning up." Confronted the heart of the matter.

"Uncle, I have listened to how you met and married aunty Madelyn. It is heartbreaking what you have endured. But leaving Luce is going to tear you guys apart. I can see cracks open in the family. Look, I need you. They need you. Hold it together. We can ride this one out. Grandma is giving up. If you want aunty to get an apology from her, the best chance is to stay in Luce. She's not leaving. She told you that herself." I sounded wise for a change. Maybe the age thing was getting to me.

Uncle Joe sat back and folded his arms at me. "No one owes you anything, Chris. How people treat you doesn't matter. It's your response to them that does." He went on,

"Chris, understand this; we love you. And I think Izzy is in love with you too⋯." He paused and then, "She waited on you all these years to make up your mind. Amanda was no good to you. But did you see Izzy fall apart because of it? No, instead, she occupied herself. She accepted your choices. Sometimes, you must see that everyone has choices, and they're not necessarily going to line up with yours. Not saying that you do not know this by now but that you should accept this reality." He was adamant. "You are a strong young—man. Your father did the best for you. Being an adult also means you step up to the plate." Where was all this coming from?

"Izzy, maybe hoping you provide a clear direction for yourself and hers. That's what manhood is all about." He ended the conversation and cast the line back into the pond's center.

There was silence. Then he started back up, “Madelyn and I are getting old. Everything you heard me say was to show you that there is more to people than meets the eye. We all have stories. Mostly sad ones. But if you ever look inside, you'll find that people stay with those they love. Not because they are happy or sad. Life is not a choice. Everything else is. Grandma Isabel may never ask Madelyn for forgiveness, and that's okay. When you heard her blame us for not doing well the other night, it was a projection of her failures, not ours. See, Grandma never believed Madelyn would ever turn out good.” He paused, “But what Grandma doesn't see is that Madelyn is an exact replica of her marriage to grandpa. She sided with him instead of her daughter, making Madelyn's life a living hell. She had a choice to support her daughter in that time of need. But chose not to. In her own mind, she thinks that Madelyn is doing the same thing with me." Uncle Joe had a lot on his chest···

"When I decided to shut down the café, it was final. And yes, Madelyn must follow my lead. I'll take care of her till I die. She'll go with me to Florida and spend time with the other side of the family." I learned an important lesson listening to him that day. I finally figured it out. A man was willing to go it alone when necessary. Win or lose.

My whining annoyance created room for a learning experience. Uncle Joe never allowed room for a rebuttal. He always taught me that owning up to every situation is how one should live a proper life.

"Which is why I'm going to need you to understand quickly because I have a favor to ask you. It's probably the most important thing I've ever asked you." He shifted gears in our conversation—awkwardly. But it worked, for he captured my undivided attention.

"Here's the card to someone I need you to contact. Priscilla Williams, she goes by Perry. She's a business owner and a former modeling—scout agent." He flicked the card across the wooden bench to my side.

"I've known her for a while, and she's fond of Izzy. She wants to take her in and possibly··· Help her start a modeling career." he said.

I took the card and studied the holographic lettering on it. The logo design and wording gave an immediate impression of perfection. I looked at uncle Joe to continue the conversation…

"Izzy cannot be dragged down the path she's on with the family. She's been through a lot with her parents. She's letting her life pass her by. It's not fair to her. I think she needs a fresh start. Modeling will do it for her. At least for now. She's a good girl Chris. Don't mess this up. Her dad will literally kill you. Not trying to scare you, if you know what I mean." He said.

"What do you mean her father will kill me? I was curious. I didn't do anything."

"Chris, sometimes, I tell you, boy, you play too much. I know you like her just as much. And you expect her father not to lay down ground rules when he finds out. You better not do something stupid. I will be the first one on your throat." He firmly replied.

"Oh···huh! I got it, Uncle Joe." I figured it out. He was giving me permission to date Izzy the man—way. I got his coded message. The killing was just to ensure I took good care of Izzy.

"Does she know about this?" I had to ask.

"Know about what? The poor girl is packing her stuff like she's moving with us to Florida." He answered.

"And you not going to tell her?" Thought out loud···

"You kidding me? That's why I gave you that business card in the first place. It's your job to tell her how you feel and that you are staying with her." He threw the burden on my shoulders.

"Just so you know, your parents are also aware of this. You two should be together. Fighting the world, son. You have my permission and everybody else's." I didn't want him to say anything—anymore. How did he talk to my dad about dating Izzy? And if he did, why didn't he tell him about his financial troubles? It was too much. After my breakup with Amanda, I cried and begged for a better relationship privately. Here came an opportunity with a blessing from the most respected and loved people in my world. Was I dreaming?

I blanked out to whatever else he said after that. Strange—adrenaline flew rushingly through my body as I processed what he had told me. Is Izzy staying with me and in the same house? It felt like an arranged marriage or something along those lines, to say the least. I could see why uncle Joe was avoiding eye contact with me now. He had done his job and delivered the message on behalf of all parties involved. And here I thought, my dad was not in my life and didn't even care. This was a wild suggestion to my limited understanding. Of course, I respected and admired Izzy. There was nothing left about the situation except her acceptance of that reality.

"You'd trust her to stay with me?" He chuckled at my question.

"Not really··· her father suggested it." he looked away, shaking his head. "He's coming back in a year, and he isn't happy with where Izzy is in her life right now. He thinks this will challenge her and make her grow. The thing is, he doesn't really know it's another young—lad like yourself. He thinks it is your parents staying with Izzy." He said it with admitted guilt.

"So, you just lying to him?" And.

"We are not lying to him; no father will accept this kind of proposal directly. We are crossing our fingers and hoping you do not disappoint. See, Chris, technically, you live in your father's condo. So, it's easier to explain to her dad that you two fell in love and moved in together. You catch my drift?" He looked up and directly at me, smiling.

"Uncle Joe, you—dirty, but yep. It is what it is. A man is gotta do what a man is got to do, right?" I smiled back.

"That's my boy! I knew you had it in you." He was relieved.

"What do you mean I had it in me?" Fixated on his lure.

"Courage son, courage." He reached out for another worm, inspected his hook, and cast it back into the pond. No more—words were needed.

CHAPTER FOUR

Breakaway

I sloshed down on the hard tile at the pool's edge in the puddle of partial water and my own sweat. I collapsed against the cool tiles and gasped for air like a fish out of water. You know that feeling when your lungs are on fire, and your limbs feel like wet noodles? Yep, that was the experience times—twenty. I snatched off the goggles I wore to prevent cutting off circulation to my brain. For more air, I put my arms up to my pounding head. Josh waddled over with his wet duck—feet and kicked me on my side. I winced in annoyance but didn't bother to sit up. My soul was leaving my body at that point. Fridays were group sessions, and lots of friends and fellow competitors congregated at the pool. The event was more engaging because more eyeballs watched us swim.

"How are you not dying from those weighted laps?" I asked with half my face smashed against the pavement as I rolled to my stomach. This technique worked for me. It revolved around the idea that if I stayed on the floor and kept my body turning in different positions, my recovery time would be cut in half. Well, it worked, but my coach was against it. You can imagine how angry he must have been whenever I did it. Good news though, it worked every time.

"When you've swum as many marathons as I have, your body becomes numb to all forms of pain." Josh sipped from his water bottle.

"You should join me in the morning for a jog soon, yeah···get that stamina back up—eh! What say you?" He jabbed me in the shoulder blade with his elbow. I cringed in pain and flipped my head to the other cheek as my hair whipped—into droplets.

"I wouldn't go running on my own free will if you handed me one hundred right now. Let alone wake up early." I glared up at him from the floor. He drizzled water from his bottle into my ear. I jerked up and shook my head profusely.

"It wouldn't matter anyway; you probably have one hundred dollars in your couch cushions right now." And he was probably right. He sipped again.

Josh is one of those friends that I only saw in group sessions. He was ill-mannered and blatantly honest. Practically everyone talked about him and seemed not to care at all. Being ranked second to me statewide bloated his ego, pending an explosion. He had it in him to beat me, but his ego stood in the way. We were opposites. I was extremely patient. To him, patience was a foreign language. At the pool were six swimmers, two coaches, and Jordan, who occasionally volunteered to help. Jordan was an ambitious young swimmer. He wanted to join the elite program but had not been enrolled. Like many swimmers, he knew getting accepted to the program meant an instant shot at a successful swimming career.

Usually, you would be scouted to get in, which is how I was accepted. But you could also request to be trailed into acceptance by the program organizers. Trailing in our world was signing up for as many tournaments as possible. Scouting agents keep an eye on your performance. If you continuously ranked 1st—5th, chances were very good you could be recruited. The thing is it took about 2 years for the process to complete. Athletes who were scouted felt privileged and openly arrogant compared to those who got in by the trial. I hated it when they bragged with nothing to show for in real competitions. It was all too—stupid to me, but I guess athletes saw competition in everything they did. Someone had to lose or win.

“What happened to the Spaniards?” Josh asked.

“Tony is an Italian dude. Jordan from Belize, they're totally different.” I said.

“In the sense that they’re both butt-kissers?” Josh sought clarification. He was a piece of work in everything he said and did.

"You never know, dude. Jordan could beat all of us any given day." I choked on my water from his remark as he laughed hysterically.

"I never said he couldn't. Speaking of Tony, though, whatever happened to him? Why did he quit mid-season?" I asked.

"He's in Europe. He lost interest in the sport. He wanted to travel, so he's gone." Josh answered.

"Seriously, that's why he left? To be honest, I thought he got a girl pregnant." I laughed.

"He's got a lot of girls, but I'm pretty sure he didn't get any of them pregnant. Can't vouch for him now, though; it's been over a year since I last heard from him."

"That's not a smart move on his part to quit the sport after so many years. Wasted time—energy. He could've traveled after making some money. Waited··· you know what I'm saying?"

"Couldn't agree more." He sighed.

Josh rested his back on his elbows, his short blonde hair stuck to his forehead. I shrugged in response and kicked the water looking over the pool as we waited on the coaches to line us up for the next exercises...

***

Later that evening, I decided to be a homebody; I cooked dinner, ate, washed up, and dove into my duvet. I had not heard from Izzy all day, so I decided to check on her. Not wanting to make it obvious, I called aunt Madelyn instead.

"Just checking up on things to see how far we've gone with the prep," I said.

"All is well, Chris. I know you want to talk with Izzy, right?" She was direct.

"Yes, that too···." I had been called out.

"Uh huh···"

"What···aunty." I Felt—shy.

"Chris, we haven't left yet. And your appetite is on a high already?" She went on, "Should I be worried?" Before I could chime in, "You not gonna be giving me a grandbaby before I settle in Florida, are you?" Okay···was that a question? I waited for more info. There was silence.

"Woo—woo, aunty. It's not like that. Seriously I was just checking up on you." Laughed. Aunty hid her pain so well. You could've thought she had kids of her own.

"Make sure her room is set. We should be there in a couple of hours." She finished.

"Will do," I replied. But was I ready?

Her room was directly across from mine, and Madelyn was familiar with the condo. She knew the place had enough space to live comfortably.

"You haven't brought up moving into Izzy yet, have you?" She asked

"No··· why?"

"Were you not going to tell her?" she sighed again.

"W-wait; why? You plan to tell her tonight on your way here, right?" I thought this was cruel. I rolled over to my side, propped by the headboard for lumbar support.

"She's going to freak out! I don't get it. Why won't you just tell her now?" I missed their logic entirely.

"You know how she is, Chris! If we tell her there's no way on earth she will go through with it as a matter of fact," she paused for a moment and lowered her voice, "I just had a talk with her. I kind—of suggested the idea of her staying in Luce when we move; talk about dead on arrival···." Aunt Madelyn continued, "She's missing her mother, Chris. So, the idea of going back to Florida has sparked the angst in her to go as well." She waited for my reaction. That suddenly made my stomach dip with nervousness. What if Izzy hated living with me? What if she smacked me in the face after getting dropped off and ran away to Florida. It was stupid to think that far out, but she could've hated living in Luce. Maybe she thought they'll make her stay at grandma's house. I couldn't blame her. The place was left back in the 1800s.

"I raised Izzy and know her best. She's conflicted between being close to her mother and pursuing her own dreams." Madelyn continued, "But she's not a little girl anymore. We've got to push her to stand on her own two feet, and if I tell her now, she won't go through with it." This time I sighed into the phone, "You're right. Let's see when she gets here." I was defeated by the complexity; the situation had taken. On one hand, uncle Joe said, I will be the one to tell her on another, Aunty was in full panic. Were they on the same page when it came to Izzy?

"I'm sure you will do just fine," Aunty said with sarcasm.

"What's that supposed to mean?" I chuckled.

"I'm sure you'll do everything to guarantee to live with a pretty girl." she laughed out loud.

"Aunty, have I ever told you that you and uncle Joe was meant to be from birth?" I waited for her response…

"What did you say?" Her pitch went up.

"Oh yep, that got your interest. You guys are pushing us together. You tug—teaming." I couldn't get my words out, and we both laughed.

"You sure seem to think that Joe and I don't see how you cozy when together." She deflected my rather direct observation.

"What do you mean?" I scoffed.

"Yeah, your googly eyes and what—not. Those giggling and nudging each other, we see it." Aunty had ways with her words. Sometimes she came off childishly, but that was her. We had come to accept. What did googly—giggly mean? Especially coming from an adult. I loved aunty very much. She had been there for Izzy and me regardless of what we went through.

"You mean being friends and having conversations?" I played innocent.

"So, you're telling me you're not attracted to Izzy?" She waited for my answer. I wanted to take the 5th on that one, but I blew it.

"I like her."

"No···you love her, Chris. Never like a woman. Always love a woman." She was firm. I was a little shocked. Had I hit a nerve accidentally with aunty?

"That's not what I asked you, though," she replied.

"Chris, we honestly appreciate everything you do for us. We don't take it lightly." She choked up. Her emotions were very much so on the surface. The only logical conclusion had to be the move to Florida.

I remembered my mother not wanting to leave the condo after years of pestering dad about needing a bigger space. Maybe women get attached to places like that or the city, the people, and stuff. Either way, my job was to be there and help lighten the burden.

"That's all I'm saying." she laughed between sobs, "Anyway, I'll be over there with Izzy in a few." Silence···radio sounds in the background.

"Alright, I'll see you then," I replied.

We ended the call. I dropped the phone on the bed and fell face—down on it. In a few moments, I was to have a roommate. The irony was how Amanda had hurt me so badly, I thought I, and relationship would never work. At least the pain told me so. I hardly knew that the possibilities of love lay a few months out. And all I had to do was hang in there. What would Amanda do if she found out that Izzy and I had moved in together? And that wasn't even the worst part; we were dating. At that moment, I realized Amanda had never uttered the words when it was over between us. Yet it felt and looked like a breakup. She had been gone, never called or clarified anything. So, was it right to assume our relationship was over and for good?

She also wanted to move in with me at one point, but my mother was totally against it. When Amanda learned my mother was against the move, she lost it. In hindsight, I think that move was designed to trap me. On more than one occasion, she claimed that my condo was the perfect spot for us to start our lives together.

Talking of which, her attitude and mannerism changed around the same time. She grew colder—meaner, and more distant. The lapse since she left allowed me to reflect and process everything that transpired during our relationship. How did I miss that? Even though I had heard her claims, it was a sign that we were not meant to be unless my mother okayed us living together. She may have been manipulating me to muzzle herself into my life. My dreamy-self could not listen to the red flags. I kept beating a dead horse. I thought we could build a strong relationship, pursue our goals, and later move in together. Was I wrong? Sure, we patched our relationship, and many times, it ran purely on fumes of hope until the wheels came flying off at the airport.

Down—deep, I had strong feelings for Amanda even though my anger and resentment had somewhat subsided. Often than not, I recalled the good times, especially vacations we took together. Yeah, lots of memories. But I had to let that go. Izzy was here now. We were going to create new ones together. Was I worried? Was I self-sabotaging? You bet but my anxiety, mixed with excitement at the prospect of staying together, had me twisted mentally. Didn't know if it was time to celebrate a milestone or worry about an eventual short-lived relationship with Izzy.

CHAPTER FIVE

New Beginnings

Isabelle Kaia Ingram

It was a Saturday morning and nine-forty to be exact, when I woke up. Late was not even a word. Everyone must have been worried at the café.

Izzy had stepped up to the roommate challenge, seemed in control, and took charge. I was in trouble, no doubt. My thoughts were on Uncle Joe. What did he think about my tardiness? This was my first night with Izzy, and I had disaster written all over it. If this was a test, I would have flunked for sure. How could he trust me to take care of Izzy if I couldn't get her to work? Let alone on time?

I rose up, pushed the comforter from my face, and saw a note by my lamp stand, with a mug beside it. I reached for the note, and it read; Sleepy wake up! I'm catching the bus. See you at the café.

"What! Izzy had left already?" I thought out loud. She didn't bother to wake me up and just left a note? This didn't look good on me from a first impression. Here I found myself passed out with no regard to my work schedule. I was supposed to drive her there. And why didn't she just wake me up? Maybe pouring ice water on my face or something could've worked. I worried about uncle Joe's thoughts, especially if I was good enough to fend for us. Izzy had to catch a bus not to be late. I felt like crap at the thought. What a shame. Could Izzy think that I cared for Amanda more than her? Oh wait, we were not officially dating. And if that was the case, had I ruined my chances? Talk about self-sabotaging. I sat up on the side of the bed and stretched for the mug. The contents were hot chocolate. She had cared to fix me a hot drink but not wake me up. She was indeed different from Amanda, no question.

I sipped the hot contents, tasted pretty good. Just like I wanted. I got to my phone and sent her a text, "On my way, so—sorry." I jumped in the shower, lathered up quickly, and rinsed. Redeeming myself and saving face was a priority.

***

"Morning!" I wrapped my arm around her shoulders, snapping her out of her thoughts. She turned around and watched me enter the kitchen to put up my things. She stared a little longer than I expected. What was she thinking? Lazy dude···

Izzy snapped her head back to the dishes sharply as I turned around. Ms. Amber chuckled at me in the distance. She was the only one who knew about my feelings for Izzy at work outside of my uncle and aunty. It's not like I had a choice in telling her. She caught me staring way too often and put two and two together. I was held at the mercy of her ability to keep a secret. I could only trust her maturity and not to say a word. So far, it has been so good.

"You need help with the dishes?" I leaned against the other side of the sink and folded my arms.

"Uh, not really. I think uncle Joe wanted you in the office, though." She kept her eyes on the sink and maintained her nonchalant look. I walked off to the office. It wasn't even the fact that she liked me that made me anxious, but my fears. We don't get to choose love; love chooses us. When I returned from seeing uncle Joe, who was basically just worried, Izzy had finished washing the dishes and stood with Ms. Amber for a quick chat. I could guess that she was getting schooled on the varieties of dinners to make at home. Ms. Amber enjoyed homemaking. Talked about her man, children, and one grandson. I felt sorry for the poor guy. He must have listened to so many stories of her days at work to no end. Possibly grew old or perpetually fell asleep at the dinner table in boredom. Your guess would be as good as mine. And that was not even a stretch of the imagination.

She gawked about when she was younger and had a better body and how it felt when she first fell in love. I shuffled into the restaurant's lobby, arms full of condiments and table menus. I couldn't help but hear them. They were loud; I did not eavesdrop— seriously. If it helped Izzy, that's all that mattered to me.

"Izzy!" I shouted.

"Yes!" She shouted right back, literally, at the back of my head. I jumped a little. She laughed. I didn't know she had been trailing me all that time.

"Can you help me organize these?" I splashed the contents over the tabletop. Well, there was nothing unusual about setting up tables. It was part of our morning routine at least an hour before we opened the café. I grabbed what I needed for the table at the far corner of the lobby.

"Wait," she called after me. "I'll swab the tables before you put that stuff on there; they need to be cleaned." She told me while on her heels to grab cleaning agents. I leaned against booth cushions and hid my appreciation of her with my tougher—outer shell. Deep down, though, I knew she was happy we had gotten closer. And maybe, just maybe, the talk in the café could shift to, "Izzy falls in love with a handsome heir of a real estate empire." We were no longer just—friends. I thought our emotions must have been broken loose by that first kiss at her grandma Isabel's house. Talking of grandma, I wondered how she was doing. I decided I would call her later that evening.

Izzy crossed over to swab the next table and distracted my train of thought. I followed her with three sets of stuff to put on it.

"Chris, sweetheart! Come over and help us lift these crates out of the hallway." The ladies called in the back. I don't think Izzy liked that at all. She got jealous.

"Why did they call you sweetheart? That's overboard." Izzy muttered.

"I heard that," I said, smiling at her.

"You better end it soon too." She was furious.

"Are we···are you···saying what I think you are saying?" I moved closer.

"Go help your girlfriends at the back. They miss you···" she shoved me.

"My eyes are on you," I said, feeling her jealous empathically. It made me happy.

Izzy pulled her self—loathing card. "It is supposed to be your heart, not your eyes." She lectured, "Anyways, go help your women. While at it, flex your biceps. They like that too..."

"Oh yeah··· get a divorce from them before proposing to me." She smiled and kept swabbing.

"Copy that, your highness. Let me go file with the courts." Izzy and I were the youngest people at the café.

The sunlight inched across the room as morning turned into afternoon. The place was—packed. Uncle Joe had not told anyone besides his family that he was closing the café for good. He was busy planning some type of closing celebration. Obviously, I was not on board with that idea. But who was I? Their best friend's kid. Right?

We swung the doors open, and the shop was ready for business. Soon our coffees and teas were being served. I couldn't help but notice a new face walking in. She stood out from the rest of our usual crowds. She may have been in her early thirties and was well-kept. She wore a shortened blonde hairstyle, a navy-blue suit with frills at the end of her skirt, and blazer sleeves.

"Good morning, Welcome to Paradise. How may I serve you? Coffee? It's good." I gave her my best smile.

"What's in the coffee?" She looked directly into my eyes.

"Well, it's the best coffee in the world. A blend of East African and South American." Wanted to sound very knowledgeable.

"Okay, don't know much about blends. But make me a cup. Cream—sugar, natural everything." She was standoffish.

"Coming right up." I smiled courteously.

Izzy eyed our conversation from across the counter. I walked over to her.

"A cup of coffee, everything natural, like organic." I gave her a smile and patted the top of her hand.

"Yeah, whatever…" she pulled her hand away.

"What? We are serving customers." Not convincing enough.

"I hear you."

"What do you mean?"

"Well, I think it depends on if they are hot chicks, right? And for the record, she's got miles on her." She frowned.

"Meaning age?" I asked. No answer.

"Come—on, Izzy, she's a professional lady. Maybe she's used to getting things done her way. Besides, we are like amateurs in a coffee shop to her." I lamented.

"I don't think she's from here," I added. Possibly insulted Izzy more with my comments. Oh, poor me. Could I do anything right with women?

"Izzy, please, make this easy on me today," I begged.

"Okay, you get the pass; if we were not moving back to Florida, I would've been the meanest girl you ever dated." She half—smiled.

"Huh! Did you say···" I was caught flat-footed.

What did Izzy mean? I thought her uncle and aunty had told me she was staying with me. She had brought some stuff over. What? I was confused. Hadn't she just not spent the night at my condo? I needed answers, and I needed them quick.

I stormed into uncle Joe's office.

"Hey Chris," he smiled, "What can I do with this flyer, you like it?" He was busy turning it around upside—down. I just stood there feeling cheated and misled.

"Uncle, what's the deal with Izzy?" I vomited anger.

"What deal···is everything okay. I mean, last night was not?" He was equally surprised.

"I thought you told me that she was staying in Luce. Well, she just told me she's leaving with you folks for Florida. Okay, I'm either lost, or something is wrong with my brain. Tell me I'm not crazy?" Catching my breath.

"Ohh···I thought you understood that we could not tell her she was staying. All she knows is that she can stay at your place when she visits Luce. So yesterday, we convinced her to at least try out a night. We also told her that whenever she comes to town, you'll let her spend at your condo." He was slow, as if holding critical intel from me.

"Okay, let me get this straight. Are you saying she's moving with you folks or not?" I demanded an answer.

"No, I said, Chris, that you can convince her to stay in Luce if you want her to. Did you think···" I didn't wait to hear the rest. I walked out, slamming the door behind me.

"Chris! Come here···" uncle Joe yelled out my name. And for the first time as long as I had known him, I disobeyed···

CHAPTER SIX

The night before the move

__Izzy__

There was a knock at the door while I worked on my latest sketch.

"Come in!" I called. Aunt Madelyn peeped her head through the door. She walked over to the bed and sat near my knees.

"Is that your shoreline drawing?" she asked me. I nodded and turned the book towards her. She smiled in approval, then paused for a second.

"So, are you ready for the move tomorrow?"

I shrugged a little. "I mean, yeah, I guess."

"You're not upset about leaving your friends?" she scooted closer.

"Not enough to stop the move." I was direct.

I continued to draw without looking up. Aunty knew I had trouble connecting with "friends" outside of work. I felt like my friends were closer to each other than they were to me. I doubted they'd miss me. She reached out and wrapped her arms around me, resting her head on mine. I took a moment from sketching and hugged her back.

"Izzy, I want you to know this. Sometimes life changes suddenly with no questions asked. If you pull—back, you'll be left behind. You must roll with the punches." she said. I appreciated her pep—talk, but it was corny. If that had been the case, they should've stayed and saved the café.

"So, when tomorrow comes and it's time to say goodbye. Don't be scared or nervous. The path we're on will only grow us into better people." she held my cheeks.

She must've been talking about saying goodbye to Chris. She knew for certain I liked him. I sighed with embarrassment but agreed with it to make things move— faster. She gave me one last hug before saying goodnight and walked out of my bedroom. I was left in the company of my own creativity. The truth was that I wanted to do more than just hang out with him. I loved Chris. The few months we had been around each other after his breakup with Amanda opened my heart to him. For years my stability came from family and art. I hadn't been in a relationship that could've given me another perspective on life. I was okay with moving to Florida but was equally distressed about not seeing Chris. I wanted to kill that emotion in me. But at the same time, it felt like I would be losing a great stab at love. Deep down, I had my own doubts about ever meeting Mr. Right. Maybe I had settled for whatever life threw at me and had not fought hard enough for myself. I was stuck in the middle of desires and wants. Couldn't tell you if my life was better or worse. But this much I knew, I cared deeply for my family and had fallen in love with Chris. Anything else was foggy at best.

I had avoided looking over my reality. My twenties had caught with me. Had not joined college; my job was as a barrister at my uncle's café, and now drove underwater.

My mother was mentally ill and a soldier for a dad. What was the purpose of all this? Was I abandoned or not accepted? I wondered why dad never realized that mom had mental challenges before bringing me into this world. But again, how was I supposed to be born? Part of me was proud of my genetics—beauty and all. The other wasn't that appealing. I had lived life behind closed doors to the outside world. Endured the hardship of making mental notes to avoid talking about my parents. Had done it throughout my schooling years. Living with my grandma was not necessarily attractive, to say, around friends. Everyone seemed to talk about their parents, siblings, and vacations. Was I alive? If yes, to what extent?

I was lost in my picture—drawing when my phone chimed. Glancing over, I saw it was Chris. The text flash read; *Go outside and check on our tree.* I had named the tree Tim. I remember him laughing at the idea of giving a tree a name. But with time, he came to accept it. Even enjoyed calling him Tim as well.

So why would he not just call me? I wanted to hear his voice. I needed Chris to need me. Why was he not fighting for me, all the life, I longed for the man I fell in love with to fight for me. Deeply I wished the text could've read; *I'm outside.* And if I opened my window from my upstairs bedroom, I would see him with flowers and on one knee begging me not to leave Luce. I would've stayed if he had asked me to. Even if it meant living with Grandma.

I was in my pajamas; it was eleven an hour to midnight. Caught in a tug of war, I asked if I could go outside per his instructions or stay in defiance of him not calling me. What if he was letting me go forever! He had no idea that I loved him. Had I played too hard to—get beyond saving? I knew he was visibly upset with his uncle when he stormed from the café earlier. But why was I getting punished? Chris did not want to talk with anyone at the time. I watched him drive off. It was a repeat of what he had done at the house when things had fallen apart. I wanted him to talk. But it was not going to pressure him, especially at the café with guests. The last thing everyone needed was a spectacle of a new version of the "family feud," as grandma had rightly called it.

I seriously longed for him to call me. He hadn't, and uncle Joe didn't say a word about it either. On the way home, we stayed clear of the subject. I kept glancing at my phone in the hope that he would eventually call me. Not even a text, and when he did, it was about the tree···Tim. What now? It was too much for me. My heart was torn. I knew he cared for me but didn't think he was aware; I felt the same.

Chris was not about to leave me like that. I told myself, but again···silence had taken a toll on me.

"He better not be out there by the tree," I said to myself. I planned to slap him first, then cry and tell him I loved him. Curiosity got me speeding down the stairs; I violated the possibility that I could wake up grandma. I was not sure if my aunty left or stayed for the night. I met Tim in his usual state, steady as ever in the yard. Winds majestically swayed his branches as the leaves danced in the harmony with the waves. It was beautiful seeing crickets pop through the grass. The air was fresh and carried a light chill in it. I could hear a chatter of night critters in the distance. Felt like music without rhythms.

Suddenly I noticed an envelope taped on his trunk and read; To Tim's Mother. I hurriedly drained the contents···

Dear Izzy,

I'm writing to you concerned about Tim. He just informed me that you are moving away tomorrow, leaving us behind. Since Tim will be staying with a new family when you move, he will miss your hugs. You know too well without those hugs, he may not live long···his days are now numbered. But he has requested that you honor one more wish...

In the little—blue bag are sugar maple seeds. Grow his little brother or sister while in Florida. Call us when you do. You owe us that much. See you···

PS He requested Tina for a sister or Thomas for a brother.

The look I wore clutching those seeds was a giddy—mess. I laughed and hugged Tim. Bittersweet, I felt deep inside. Chris cared for what I cared for. Suddenly the veil that held my bounds together ripped apart. A surge of an emotional pang and desperation to be with him rose up inside. I had no idea what it felt like to love and want to be with someone that badly. My childhood dream of falling in love with a handsome man came to life. If I left Luce, he would be gone when I returned from Florida to visit. He was heartbroken, and I was playing a bigger part in destroying the little hope he had in women. His parent's marriage was not perfect, just like my parent's marriage. But at least my mother was sick. He was healthy and normal on all accounts. They chose not to get along. Chris had been denied a healthy view of a good family. The little he knew about love, he freely gave it to Amanda and then to me. It was his best. To be honest, he tried. I knew it, felt it, and even held it. I touched my lips where his kiss was planted and my hips where his massive arms once squeezed. I missed him. No way! Warm drops of tears rolled out and then streamed.

“I love you, Chris. Please call me. Please call me···say it's not over.” I hang up after calling his cellphone three—times and going straight to voicemail. My voice shook between sobs···

To be continued···

Bora' Nyree is an actor and modeling student.

She writes for fun and education.

www.ingramcontent.com/pod-product-compliance
Lightning Source LLC
La Vergne TN
LVHW010548160826
845677LV00013B/3047

* 9 7 9 8 8 8 9 5 5 8 7 4 3 *